In the Space Between

(Stories & Sketches)

by

Lee Sloan
Adian Suvic
Aaron Joiner

River Boat Books

Printed in the United States of America.
Published by River Boat Books, St. Paul, MN.
First printing January 30, 2025

ISBN: 978-1-955823-19-7

Cover artwork adapted from the painting *Head on a Stem* by Odilon Redon circa 1900.

Nenne mir Dein Verhältnis zum Schmerz,
und ich will Dir sagen, wer Du bist!
— Ernst Jünger

Sage mir Dein Verhältnis zum Sein, falls Du überhaupt
davon etwas ahnst und ich sage Dir, wie Du Dich und
ob Du Dich mit "dem Schmerz" "beschäftigen" wirst
oder ob Du ihm nachdenken kannst.
— Martin Heidegger

Words have no power to impress the mind without the
exquisite horror of their reality.
— Edgar Allan Poe

Special thanks to our friend Torin for his supportive presence throughout the creation of this anthology!

A NOTE FROM THE PUBLISHER

This slim volume contains the work of three young, emerging authors, and by young I mean they are all in their twenties. They are working on their craft, which is why I felt it important to publish them. They need to see their work in print, visible, tangible, rooted in time and place. All of these stories (some are what I would call sketches) reflect a very specific Gothic sensibility characterized by an exploration of psychological isolation and an appreciation for a palpable even visceral terror that blurs the line between the real and the imaginary. And yet each author focuses on decidedly different aspects of what Gothic literature is or might become.

Lee Sloan embraces a world where reality, often reflecting physical deformity, is shaped by bizarre even brutal accidents which rob the characters of some vital aspect of their humanity but which in turn give us, the reader, a glimpse into some universal truth about what it means to be human, a truth which makes the reader care. In this, Mr. Sloan is like a young Stephen King. Indeed, his story "Savannah Abernathy's New Truck" reminds me of King's short story "One for the Road," at least on a structural level.

Adian Suvic's Gothic sensibility is more European in his focus on how we communicate with others and with ourselves about the nature of the reality where we find ourselves. "The Stories We'd Tell" is as much about the destructive power of language to reframe how we think of those we love the most (or should love) as it is about what we must do to survive the damage inflicted upon us by our families. For Mr. Suvic, language becomes a surgeon's scalpel for dissecting memory and dreams and reminds me in some ways of writing of Daphne du Maurier. Compare the opening line of du Maurier's novel *Rebecca* ("Last night, I dreamt I went to Manderley again.") to the opening line of Mr. Suvic's short story "It Comes Back" ("I've been having weird dreams—ones that I don't think are mine.").

Aaron Joiner is perhaps the most traditional (i.e. early 20th century) of these three young authors in his approach to creating a Gothic landscape. The sense of mystery, of mood and suspense that he creates in his short story "The Holes on Ashdale Mound" reminds me of the symbolic almost preternatural landscape (or mindscape, if you will) of Richard Connell's "The Most Dangerous Game."

So let me offer you these twelve stories from three young writers who are working on their craft. The stories they have written here go beyond the words on the page and reveal

what Heidegger called the pain of being, a pain
borne of the fact that life itself is essentially
fatal, and yet here we are. We live our lives
in the space between (hence the title of this
collection) as best we can. These stories reflect
that uncomfortable truth. They are, one could
say, remarkably honest. And to be honest is all
you can ask of any writer, at any age.

Peter Damian Bellis
December 31, 2024

In the Space Between

Between

(Stories & Sketches)

CONTENTS

Orbit
by Lee Sloan

When I saw the rabbit, it was dragging itself
in small, desperate circles within a muddy ditch
near the Braxton Road exit. Its right back foot
was crushed and towed behind, tendons and
muscle fibers pulling taut with each rock it
snagged on. I knew the rabbit needed help, but
the lurid sight hindered my ability to move. My
attention had shifted from the need to change
a tire, which had blown a few hundred yards
back, to a forlorn situation.

A car whizzed by, and its beaming blue
headlights snapped me into action. I swallowed
hard and bent to pick up the rabbit. The mistake
was not lifting the rabbit, but the speed at
which I did. The creature's mouth twisted into
a small circle of pain, and it wailed out into the
night. The sound—a sharp, demanding squeal—
startled me. The rabbit's ruined foot bounced off
my arm. I shuddered.

The night was brisk, but the creature needed
my sweater more. I carefully swaddled the
rabbit, being cautious of the foot, and tucked it
away in the passenger seat. I completed the tire
change, listening for sounds of distress from my

new passenger. Back now in the car, emergency
lights still flashing, I stared at the piteous animal
beside me. The rabbit was tiny and eggshell
white. It was cute now that the macabre foot
was hidden away. Dusky eyes peered into mine,
pleading with me to lick its wounds and forever
lift it from the ditch—so I did.

*   *   *   *   *   *

The rabbit responds to Orbit, a name I felt
fitting after watching him (I'm pretty sure it's
male) haul himself in little death ellipticals just
two weeks ago. Orbit has since been living the
good life. I feed him a special blend of rabbit
food and veggies daily—he has taken a special
liking to celery—and built a play area in the
backyard where he has a smattering of toys and
things to chew on.

The mutilated foot, after a few nights of me
not knowing what to do, detached from the rest
of Orbit and wilted. I'll admit, I was afraid to
take him to a vet because I know how expensive
they can be, so I opted for a few cheap toys
and a doggie bed and held onto hope that the
foot wouldn't become a problem. The limb was
a terrible sight, but never appeared infected. I
found it in Orbit's bed, without Orbit, crusted
into the fabric.

I pulled it from the fabric, listened to what
sounded like Velcro pulling away from cotton,

then examined it in my hand. I smirked. The unluckiest rabbit's foot in the world. I opened the trashcan, ready to dispose of the foot, but ended up placing it on the counter instead. I couldn't get rid of it.

*   *   *   *   *   *

Orbit became my best friend. Whatever I was doing, Orbit was nearby. His ability to hop was partially disabled by the missing foot, but he did the best he could with sloppy, sideways hops that were as adorable as they were humorous. I didn't let him sleep in my bed, even though he wanted to and demonstrated this with persistent nightly protests of pulling on my bedsheets with long rabbit teeth. I was afraid I might roll over and suffocate him in my sleep; I was a heavy sleeper. So, his bed was on the floor close to my own. Whenever I was getting ready to turn in, he dragged his doggie bed into my room. This routine was my favorite.

Working from home was now exciting. Orbit made surprise visits to my desk, thumping a hind leg on the floor next to my chair until I dropped him in my lap. Taking calls for a health insurance firm was an easy job, but not so much when Orbit trounced across my keyboard and closed a customer's account mid-call. But I wasn't angry at him. I pictured him as my little secretary.

Over the years, I grew apart from friends. Some of them had kids and fell out of touch. I missed them. I wouldn't go so far as to say that I was depressed before Orbit, but bored, maybe even approaching lonely. Being in my forties and having no prior luck with relationships, I accepted my fate of being single for the foreseeable future.

Orbit changed everything. My days were now filled with warmth, making the coldness I felt before all too evident.

*　　　*　　　*　　　*　　　*

Our rituals stayed about the same, and Orbit's sporadic energy made the days short and jovial. I loved Orbit, and after almost six months, I was afraid to lose him. I became more careful with household items I deemed dangerous for him to get a hold of. I even stopped letting him come into the kitchen whenever I was cooking dinner for fear of a knife falling off the counter and piercing him.

One night, when preparing to carve a ham, one of my stainless-steel knives found its way into my foot. Initially, I hadn't noticed the long blade jutting out of the top of my foot because my eyes darted about for Orbit. I had to know he was safe. The pain set in when I was sure he wasn't around. My foot was oozing blood onto the linoleum.

I pulled the knife from my foot—cried out—and wiped away a viscous layer of blood. I was trying to see how bad the wound was underneath. Losing balance, I hobbled over and grasped for the counter. Some of my blood smeared onto the smooth marble, and one of my fingers brushed against the now mummified rabbit's foot, besmirching it with a glaze of blood. My head was spinning, but my eyes, perhaps blinded by pain, saw the foot absorb the blood as if it were thirsting for it.

I watched Orbit awkwardly round the corner. A thought hammered its way into my head; it told me Orbit knew I touched the foot. Knew I tainted it. Orbit's luminous black eyes went from the blood puddle, the site of the accident, to where I was leaning against the counter. The pain roared up my leg and into my head, erasing the peculiar thought. Weakness overcame me, and I gripped the counter harder, knuckles white. I smiled through the pain at Orbit. In jest, I asked him if he could drive me to the hospital. For an instant, I wished he could. Ambulance rides are pricey.

I cursed myself for being in this situation. The bleeding wouldn't stop, even with the numerous paper towels I was pressing against the wound. I sighed and absorbed more blood with another wad of paper towels. I had opened a sluice gate in my foot.

I looked over at Orbit, who was still

watching the predicament unfold, and I decided I had no choice but to go to the emergency room. My wallet knew an ambulance was out of the question.

Orbit hopped out of the way as I went to get my socks and shoes. Wearing them would be painful but would help suppress the bleeding hopefully long enough for me to get to the hospital without passing out.

I pulled a sock over the marred foot, which wasn't that painful; however, fitting the shoe over it sent an echo of pain throughout my body. I startled Orbit when I wailed.

Finally, I scooped Orbit up, snatched my keys from a hook near the front door, and headed out—well, I turned back to grab the rabbit's foot, then left.

*   *   *   *   *   *

Driving had never been so painful. Each time I pushed the gas pedal, I wanted to die. What was usually a thoughtless task had turned into pure hell. The nearest hospital was five miles out from where I lived, but the throes of pain made it seem like a hundred.

In the passenger seat, Orbit slept. The little white ball flashing in and out of my peripheral vision sobered me from the agony.

Just a little bit more.

An exit sign came into view. I exhaled

through parted lips and read the words: Braxton Road. The hospital wasn't far down off the exit.

My vision hazed over for a moment, a deep shock of pain from pressing the brake vibrated throughout my body, and I changed lanes. Another flash of pain, brighter.

No. Not pain. Headlights. Bright, beaming blue headlights. The brightest I'd ever seen.

I didn't make the exit—because the semi rocketed into my car. I saw the front of the truck, then road, sky, road ... then nothing.

Blackness. Flutters of light.

The ground was muddy. Cold. I wasn't inside my car anymore. Where was my car? And Orbit?

Where the fuck was Orbit?

Was he okay? The fear of my beloved rabbit being injured, or worse, dead, gave me the energy to raise my head. My car was only a few feet in front of me, sitting at an angle, smashed to hell, windows shattered—in a ditch.

I could see Orbit. He was still inside the car. Hopping. Trapped. Had any of the glass cut him? I couldn't tell, but I needed to know.

Moving to a standing position was impossible; the pain in my foot was excruciating. How bad was it? I turned onto my side to examine the foot.

I didn't have one.

My foot, and the leg it was attached to, was a few feet away from me. It had not been cleanly severed. The leg appeared as if it were pulled away by a giant and discarded. The limb was fileted, I assumed by sheets of glass as I was ejected from the car, revealing crimson muscle veiled in blood. An aroma of metal permeated the frosty air. I could see the blood that gushed out of the shoe. The injured foot wasn't a problem anymore. I felt a chill, but wasn't sure if it was from the icy air or blood loss.

I turned again to face Orbit. His lopsided hops produced a pair of desperate black eyes over the passenger doorframe in intervals. I tried to drag myself to him. Digging my fingers into the mud, I pulled. The terrain I needed to navigate was at an incline, so force, maybe more than I had, was needed to pull myself over it. I tried and failed, sliding back into the smaller trench—a ditch within a ditch. I pulled myself around to where I started, tried again, failed, slipping back into the ditch. I repeated this. Circles. Going in circles.

A miasma of exhaustion swept over me. I lifted my head to look at Orbit—and saw something I couldn't explain.

Orbit was hopping toward me, his underside becoming dark with sludge. I observed his muddy belly before I noticed that his hops were normal. Even. Not lopsided. His body crossed a beam of light produced by one of the undamaged headlights—and I saw that he had two functioning hind feet.

With strength I found only in my imagination, I dug around inside my pocket to feel for the foot.

Gone.

My eyes had a glossy coat over them, but I could see Orbit near my remaining leg, opening his mouth.

Is he going to bite me? Is he going to eat my leg?

I closed my eyes tight to clear the fog, then reopened them, determined to make out what my rabbit was doing.

I could see now. Orbit wasn't trying to bite me. Wasn't trying to eat me. His teeth were gripping my pant leg, which had ridden up to the knee, the material tightening and loosening around my leg in little rhythms. I dropped my weary head back into the mud, euphoric now with pain and the comfort of knowing that my rabbit was trying to pull me from the ditch—I hope he can.

Veiled Tongue
by Adian Suvic

The officiant spoke Korean to my English-tongued face. He spoke fast, not just at me, but at the groom, and at the congregation, a flurry of delicate Gs and gentle Ds revving from his mouth. He slapped his olive suit, right where the heart sits, trying to communicate. I looked away when he made eye contact, choosing to judge the back of people's heads. *His is more oblong, but his thin, black hair tapers off into a triangle. He got looks from the crowd: confusion, anger, fear. Her head is pyramid-like, but her hair is in a soft, round bun. No one blinked in her direction. The crowd deemed it normal.*

Then the officiant stopped, held his squirming tongue between his teeth, and waned a smile as a brigade of best men marched down the aisle. They lined up, rough, rowdy, proud, pleased with themselves for being decent enough to be selected. They wore olive, while the women wore pomegranate. We all drove about five hours to be here, some crammed in with loud families, others alone, contemplating their own love.

She rounded the corner next, white dress,

pomegranate pearls, makeup flush on her face,
a tiny girl holding the back of her dress as the
wind threw it around like a mangled goose tail.
The groom smoothed over his pompadour and
wiped an oily hand on the back of his olive
suit–the cut fit seamlessly with his square head.
She duck-waddled up, making sure her tail
didn't get tangled with any step–the tiny girl
must have gotten scooped up by the wind and
carried away.

The officiant bent over for a small,
respectful nod to the couple. A bald spot like
an abandoned nest rooted its way into his
head. Even with his head bent, I felt his face
scrunch by the gasps. He stood straight, tried to
compose himself, and started again, launching
those dainty Gs and ginger Ds to the bride and
groom, to the congregation, to me. His speech
unwound, and he spoke to the space between
the pre-newlyweds. I still couldn't understand
him, but I heard his voice breaking. He took
off his glasses, blinked infinitely at the ground,
and whispered something to the empty air. My
English-tongue didn't understand, but my ear
caught the pomegranate stuck in his throat.

How's Your Burger?
by Aaron Joiner

The fast-food joint was relatively empty
as two tall, sharp-dressed men with identical
features sat down with burgers and fries for
lunch. They had long blonde hair, held up
with product. Their faces were smooth and
pronounced. Their business suits were the
only visible distinction between the two. One
was black, the other blue. Both wore nametag
stickers that said "HELLO, MY NAME IS: a
lawyer" in invisible ink.

"This is ridiculous," exclaimed Black
Suit, biting into his burger and refusing to
acknowledge the grease trickling down his chin.
"Ever since the government returned the judicial
system to the private sector, we've had a terrible
time making ends meet. If we don't think of
a way to draw in more business, we'll have to
close the courthouse."

"It can't be helped that people never want
to show up to our events," replied Blue Suit.
He took a fry, licked the salt off, and set it to
the side of his tray. "They're just too boring.

Nothing interesting ever happens in small towns like ours. If only there were more crimes."

"If only. How can we keep this courthouse open? Do you have any ideas?"

"Hmm ... what if we find people looking to get a divorce?" Blue Suit took another fry, licked the salt off, and set it to the side of the tray. "People love divorces. I know for a fact that all of my friends are chomping at the bit for one. That could be the fuel we need to keep things going."

"No. That won't work. Believe me, I love divorce as much as the next guy, but it seems to me that divorce is only enjoyable for the ones getting them. We need something that will entertain a jury." Black Suit reached across the table and ate one of the fries on Blue Suit's tray. "The fries here are good."

Blue Suit nodded. "They have good salt here, too."

"I know."

"How?"

"Because you said so and I trust you."

Blue Suit looked at him and, for a moment, they silently held each other's gaze.

"Well, what about a murder trial?"

"There's no need," said Black Suit, "since I already kill perfectly. We should find someone else."

"I wish there was such a person."

Black Suit sighed and shook his head,

flinging grease from his chin. "Maybe the courthouse is a lost cause. Maybe we move to the city. You know, start fresh? People murder each other there all the time. It could be a good thing."

"You know I can't. Not with the wife and kid. I promised the husband I'd look after them until he got back from vacation. There's got to be other crimes. I'm pretty sure we can get Thomas Thomas who lives on Rhode Road for tax evasion."

"Yes, but that's just us collecting for the government. Tax evaders never pay well." Black Suit paused and looked at Blue Suit's burger, not even touched. "How's your burger?"

Blue Suit thought for a moment. "It's good. It's really good."

"Mine, too. It should be criminal to have food this good."

"Maybe it could be."

Black Suit's eyes widened. "You might be on to something."

"Well, there's just one small problem," Blue Suit said, licking the salt off another fry.

"And that is?"

"We'd be criminals, too. Being fined is bad enough. Owing money to yourself is humiliating, though. I don't know how I'd show my face in public if that happened."

"It'd be good for business."

"It would be, but I still don't want to."

Black Suit sighed. "Very well. Are we done here?"

"I am."

"I am, too."

"Then let's get going."

The men abruptly rose from their seats in unison.

As the two tall, sharp-dressed men with identical features attempted to make their way outside, they were halted by a young, generically pretty woman with long, generically pretty hair.

"Excuse me," said the woman.

The two men gave each other a glance.

"I overheard your conversation at the table. I think I can help."

"Who are you?" asked Blue Suit, who was too busy checking for salt in his teeth to notice the woman's arrival.

"Oh, I'm so sorry. I should have realized you wouldn't recognize me like this. I did my hair different today. Usually, I keep it short. I'm the resolution to your story."

"I don't know what you're talking about," said Black Suit.

"It doesn't matter. What does matter is what I can do for you."

"And what can you do?"

The woman turned and looked out through the glass door in silence for a moment. When she spoke again, her voice sounded somehow distant. "My neighbor's dog has been shitting in my yard for several weeks. I'm going to kill it. Perhaps you would like to have me arrested after I do."

"Or we could have you arrested now for criminal intent."

"Whoa, whoa! Hold up," cried Blue Suit, sticking his fingers in his partner's mouth to silence him. "We'll make more if we try her after the dog's dead. Use your head, man."

Black Suit nodded, too busy sucking on his partner's fingers to speak.

"So does this arrangement work for you guys?" asked the woman, still facing the window.

"It does. What time should we have the police come by?"

"Anytime is fine. I'll have to leave the door unlocked, though, since I won't be home."

"Good, then. Ma'am, it's a pleasure doing business with you," gargled Black Suit, the fingers still in his mouth. He extended his own hand to her. The woman leaned forward and took his fingers in her mouth.

"Please, the pleasure is all mine," she gargled back.

Bendy Arm
by Lee Sloan

The first time I saw the bendy arm was a
few hours after I had been in a car accident; my
age had not yet hit double digits. The car spun
out and my head hit the windshield. Hard. Fast
forward to Clear Moorings Hospital and I was
staring at the awful spinning machine above
me—it was taking pictures of inside my head.

Everything, ultimately, was fine, and I found
myself sitting in a waiting room, staring out the
window at a dark street—which is when I saw
it. It was long, slender, and made of rubberized
skin. It waved at me. It was an oscillating,
uncanny motion, as if the arm had no business
on this earth. It vanished as quickly as it
appeared, pulled back into the void from which
it came.

Everything about that night rattled me. The
car accident. The CT scanner. But *nothing* made
the hair on the back of my neck rise and caused
little domes to inflate across my skin like seeing
that inhuman arm wave at me. When I got
home, I rested in bed and couldn't stop thinking
about it. Did I have brain damage? Was it just
a figment of my childhood imagination? Are

ghosts real? Of course, there was no way for me to answer these questions, so I eventually fell asleep with the rubbery arm coiled up like a sleeping snake in the back of my mind.

I was not a kid that scared easily. I grew up watching horror movies every other day. Trick-or-treating and visiting haunted houses excited me to no end, and never did I have trouble sleeping after being chased by blood-drenched clowns or watching slasher flicks. But, that arm ... that arm scared me to death. It flowed through my mind like blood through an artery.

A year passed. I was standing naked in front of the shower, watching the water and waiting for steam to show up—when I saw the arm again. It waved at me again, the same humanoid, undulating greeting I saw a year before, then it vanished behind the partially open rainforest curtain.

I jumped.

The reaction was involuntary. I went cold from terror, as if someone just opened a freezer door, allowing the arctic air to swaddle my body. My mind painted pictures of something horrible waiting behind the shower curtain, the elastic arm attached to it, waiting to grab me.

I knew it wasn't a movie. Knew it wasn't a special effect. The only thing I knew for sure is that it would come back.

I'm an adult now. Sometimes, I think about the car accident—how I hit my head—the last thing of note to happen before I ever saw the arm. Childhood questions rearing their ugly heads. What if something happened to my brain? A tiny bundle of neurons jostled out of place? What if I hit my head just hard enough to manifest the arm, but not hard enough for the CT machine to register any damage?

It terrifies me to think what I might have seen that night through the hospital window had I hit my head harder—what monstrous thing could have manifested, the arm just part of a greater horror. Because I know *it* would follow me, just as the bendy arm forever promises to do.

The Stories We'd Tell
by Adian Suvic

I let the air escape from my mouth, counting to three. My father was in the bar, waiting. If I stood outside for another hour, he'd be comatose drunk. Dead drunk. He's just like Billy. More accurately, Billy was like our father.

My father sat at the counter of Underbelly's with a glass of Rosie's Ruby clutched in his small, wrinkled hands. This was his spot. His and Billy's. There was a rare ambiance from this bar that others in town didn't have: the faint scent of sawdust in the air that no matter how many times you tried to inhale deeply, you couldn't get a clear enough smell. The dim blue backlight from the mirrors behind the server that muted the tone of the town. The way a compact window from the door trickled light into the bar, then once closed, immediately isolated the rest of the world from their stories.

He kept his sunglasses on even in the dull shade of the bar. I couldn't tell if he knew where to look or what was in front of him. Maybe that was why he clutched the glass so tight.

"Billy wore crocodile suits," he said. "Going

from his shoulders down to his shoes. All crocodile. The leather was caiman crocodile— every scale of it imported from Los Llanos, Venezuela. That's the blessing he needed. *All* crocodile." He let the words hang there as if that were the important part.

I hated the way his words hung. He let them hang on purpose, to taunt me. *Crocodile.* They were different from Billy's. My hands reached for the pills in my pocket. I have to talk about him. "Yeah," I said. "I think I remember the suit."

My father wiped his face. He quietly stared off as the waitress poured him another Rosie's, wetting his lips. Before she was done, he waved his hand, stopping her. "Easy, Mabel. Don't drown me. This is going to be a long night."

Mabel plunked the glass in front of my father. "You can put your barstool next to the keg if that'll make you feel better. That's what Billy did some nights."

Billy drank more or less everyday; Sunday was Mass—the day he purged himself from anything to save face. Every other day was a free buffet. Four in the afternoon; quitting time for Billy: drinking time for Billy. After harder, longer days at the recruiting office, alcohol ended up being Billy's supper. He could outdrink a fish.

"No. No, Mabel, I don't need a keg of it." My father was more than halfway through the glass before wiping his face to talk to me. "No, you wouldn't remember the suit: you were too young to remember Billy the way I do. He had this way of talking to people, of understanding what people emphasized when they spoke—the word, phrase, the—the—the thing they hung on. Billy targeted that, then talked with you—even if he had no idea what the hell the thing was."

I sat there at the counter beside him, visualizing the words he said. Billy was like that. Whether it was fishing or listening to me talk about planes, Billy would nod, eyes sparkling like a child's about to get his first round of chocolate chip pancakes. I was holding my breath again. He wanted to know. He wanted to know people, what they had experienced, what made them a person. "I think I do remember the crocodile suits. Some he got from the Orinoco River. I remember he went all the way down there himself just so he could get them. That's what I remember."

My father sighed at me. "One son dead, the other boy stupid," he said to his drink. He just focused on his Rosie's, watching the moisture roll down the side. "You don't remember the crocodile suits. They were all from Los Llanos. Billy told me long ago. Los Llanos—it's green, greener than the iguanas in Florida, greener than a shit after back-to-back plates of kale and broccoli, greener than all the money you'd ever wish to have."

For a while, I watched the moisture roll down the side, too. Mabel stood, absentminded. And I knew where her mind was. She was thinking of him. She had her own stories about Billy, ones we'd never hear. Secrets she'd never share. Maybe she also needed another bottle of pills.

I kept my mouth shut from my father. Again. I didn't want to keep feeling this way. Billy was gone. One last trip down to Venezuela and he didn't come back. No one to back me up in an argument now.

"Orinoco River," my father muttered to himself. "Hey!" He turned to me. I could almost see his eyes beyond those sunglasses. "Do you remember fishing? Do you remember when I woke you and Billy up around four to go to Johndee?"

I nodded. Of course I remembered Johndee Lake. I hated it. I hated waking up early. I hated sneaking out the house from mom. Billy did too. He'd tell me in the backseat, whispering so our father wouldn't hear: "I want to stay with mom. She wanted to make chocolate chip pancakes." His face scrunched up and his breathing got heavier with every sign that passed by. I sat in silence, waiting for my big brother to get us back home, waiting for him to say something courageous. And he did.

"Oh, the fun we had," my father said to his glass. "You have to remember fishing. The first time we all went together. I remember everything about it." He slapped his palm on the table, that faint smell of sawdust springing up again. "One more here." He swirled his glass in the air, ice clattering like teeth on bones.

"You have to be nice to those who give, lest you end up in need," he quoted some pseudo-biblical verse to the air in front of him. Maybe it was to the mirror behind the counter, luminated by those dim blue lights. "But, boy, do I wish I could relive it: the drive out there, the pine smell out the window, the warm sun on my bare arms and legs. It was everything. Everything I could give you and more."

Billy said he liked mom more. That was why our father hit him.

He looked at me. He said he had to.

On the trip to Johndee, my father pulled over off the interstate, white-knuckling the wheel, sunglasses still on, eyes focused on something vacant, far away from him. Billy and I waited in silence. Billy's face was red. I didn't think skin could get that red. A loud red. Red that reminded me of a small boy holding a red balloon in a red raincoat. Red like how my screaming throat burned.

Billy was mumbling something. He was moving his mouth, but I couldn't hear anything. It was like my eardrums blew out and I sat looking deaf and dumb at the world. A can of Rosie's Ruby Red Cider sat in the cup holder. My father grabbed it out of the cooler before he sat back down. The can cooled the heat from his palm. He cracked it open and took a sip. It must have been warm now.

"Tell me you remember it all," my father said to me in the bar, loud enough for Mabel to turn around. "We went to the creek swinging into Johndee—the one that bled into the lake."

"Yeah." My mind drifted off. I didn't care. I wanted to hit him. "I remember how it bled, how it rolled down and fell off, right at the lip."

"You *do* remember. That's right, buddy. Right off the lip of the creek into Johndee." At some angles, I could almost see the glimmer in his eye past those sunglasses. "It was a steep, steep drop; that's why I told you boys not to get too close to it. Would have damn hurt like hell and back."

Mabel set a glass of water in front of me. She saw it: the bottle in my lap. I didn't even realize I pulled it out. "Don't choke," she said. There was sympathy and guilt on her soft face.

I felt the bottle, felt the engraved *PUSH DOWN* on the lid. I was there again, holding my breath, counting to three. But I swallowed. And I said what I came here for.

"I'm burying Billy." The words lingered like Billy did. I didn't care what he had to say. "Right next to mom."

I saw his face contort, his empty eyes passed those black sunglasses. He was facing towards the back mirror, but I knew they were staring at me. The jell smoothed over his brain and out his ears as he thought of mom. He cheated on her, he hit her, he hated her. At least, that's the story Billy and I told each other.

"I thought Billy bought that spot for me. That's what he told me — that's what he would have wanted."

He would have wanted chocolate chip pancakes.

"I was supposed to be with your mother, you and Billy with your own wives. That's how it always was. That's all it ever was. Simple."

"Billy didn't have a wife."

Before the words could linger like I hoped, before he'd get this small patch of me to finally piece together who I am after these decades of not knowing a damn thing about his sons, he wet his lips and pried his mouth open.

"That's right." There was a smile that showed too many teeth on one side of his face. "Billy was single — by choice — a loner, a playboy. That's why. And you? You weren't even mine. You don't have a father."

I thought back to when we went to Johndee. The man who was not my father parked the car by the lake, close enough to skip rocks in. He held a can of Rosie's to Billy's face, chilling the burn. "That'll take your mind off it now, huh, *buddy*?" Billy sat in the passenger seat, door wide open, legs out, exposed, pink with the heat from the sun. Billy's father kept the can to Billy's cheek. It was almost like he was holding Billy down. I could tell he was eyeing me through those sunglasses.

Beyond Billy and his father, I saw it creep out from the water, trawling algae with its face. It was a crocodile, skin flaking off in the white sun, wide, flat as a pancake. Fishing wires wrapped taut around the thing's leg, causing the meat to bulge. There was blood. It leaked around the wires and down the leg. The three of us all saw it, half hissing, half wheezing at us as it dragged itself up to us.

Billy's father took the can from Billy's face and traipsed towards the crocodile. I couldn't see his expression as he moved, but I didn't have to imagine the way it contorted into that side smile showing too many teeth. There wasn't an ounce of innocence in those eyes.

The crocodile tried to flail away from him but was too fat, too wide, too weak to move away. It hissed and trudged its ugly, pathetic head. Billy's father brought the can down into the crocodile's eye, mashing it in. It thrashed, digging its tail into the murky water. He slammed his meaty hand down on the croco-dile's mouth, trapping it shut.

"Billy," his voice silk, "grab another can and come here."

The bar was closing soon. The man sitting next to me held his last glass of Rosie's Ruby, more melted ice than beer now. His wallet was on the bar counter, the black faded off into gray leather strings at the corners and folds. In the center was a washed out *I VOTED* sticker back from a time where he cared. A pair of bills fell out of the wallet and my father stared off.

You were never like Billy. And you never will be.

The crocodile lay limp on the water's edge, the man's brawny knee holding its snout to the sand. Billy gripped a cold can of Rosie's, staring at his father's red hands, mind wandering back. Billy's shoulders stiffened. His breathing stifled as if his father had covered Billy's face with a black garbage bag.

Billy inched forward, huffing. His stomach lurched. He hammered away at the crododile. The edge of the can ripped open the crocodile's eye down a few inches towards its snout. Eye meat sludged out. The crocodile tried thrashing again, but Billy's father held it in place, like he had held down Billy back in the car. The crocodile writhed and writhed until it couldn't, life slinking away. Billy tore his eyes from the pulpy meat-ooze he had created to study his father, waiting patiently, smiling, hiding something.

Then I realized there wasn't an ounce of innocence in Billy's eyes either.

Billy took what was left of the bursted can and hooked it across his father's face, ripping away an eye. There was blood. More blood than before. It flowed out into Johndee. "My boy!" he said. I stood by the car, crying, bewildered, as if

Billy had struck me instead.

"Billy was my son. Everything I wanted. A man who I could never hate." The man I once thought of as a father, long, long ago, spoke those words, to the lake of his drink, letting it linger. *I* let them linger. Not him. I walked away and let him keep telling his stories about Billy for anyone who would listen.

The Holes on Ashdale Mound
by Aaron Joiner

Growing up, I was never one to turn down an adventure. My life and all its responsibilities were quickly forgotten far too often, to an unreasonable degree, when faced with any opportunity that I deemed curious or excitable. I am relaying this bit of myself only to explain how a man making seven figures on Wall Street could abruptly leave that kind of wealth and status behind to become the sole operator and caretaker of an obscure and desolate museum deep in the hills of western Colorado.

It had been close to twenty years since leaving university life behind when I received an odd email from an old acquaintance with whom I had been initiated with into a secret society that focused on the acquisition and research of otherworldly and occult artifacts. This email detailed the history of a museum that had been erected and cared for by a number of the society's alumni. Many members had felt a need to not only preserve but to display their grotesque trophies and related research for the future generations of the society. This museum had been built on top a hill far removed from civilization, as it was understood by all involved that only those with a mental fortitude conditioned by life within the society could withstand coming into contact with these uniquely troubling relics. It was presumed that any uninitiated would, without question, go mad at such sights.

This history was imparted to me along with a plea to come out to Ashdale Mound, named by the society in honor of the primary benefactor of the museum, Trent Ashdale, a man who, even within the society, was considered to be secretive and eccentric. According to my acquaintance, the hill had been abandoned for the better part of the past year after a mysterious disappearance from one of the workers spooked the rest of the staff. I recall the electricality of my blood in that moment, an unstoppable surge that I had not felt in many years. My curiosity for the museum and its surrounding circumstances had become ravenous. I only wish now that I had given proper pause to consider that three of those who had worked at the museum had since checked themselves into psychiatric wards.

*   *   *   *   *   *

The trek to Ashdale Mound was ferociously verdant, and the hike to the museum was slow-going and miserable. I was forced to leave my vehicle behind at the highway many miles back as there was no road that would take me closer and the trees themselves seemed hellbent on keeping travelers away.

After several hours of struggling through the forest, I finally caught a glimpse of my ever-elusive destination. The museum was perched at the top of its large hill, unencumbered by any other scenery. With great effort, I lurched the remainder of the way up the slope, often stopping to rest against the trees.

I was almost at the top when I decided I could use one last rest. Night had overtaken the sky some time ago and I labored to see where my feet were stepping. As I pushed through the last few branches in front of me, I spotted a clearing up ahead. And then blackness reached up to claim me. I cried out, hands shooting out on reflex to save myself.

Terror, unlike any I had ever felt before, consumed me as I hoisted myself from that dark abyss. The sight before me, when I stood again, was unnerving and malignant. The tree line stopped abruptly where I had fallen, yielding to ground most unnatural. The soil was loose, as if recently tilled, and seemed to shimmer with an otherworldly obsidian light, faintly glistening under the moonless sky. Amid that haunting earth, holes, much like the one that I had stumbled into, were everywhere. They rose out of the dirt as far as the eye could see, the blisters of Ashdale Mound. The image of those haunting holes was my last memory of that dreadful night. Perhaps my fatigue shielded me from further disturbance of mind as I finished my ascent, for my next memory is of waking upon the front steps of the museum, deathly chilled despite the morning sun above me.

*　　　*　　　*　　　*　　　*　　　*

The next several weeks at the museum were miserable. Each night I would lie in bed praying for a dreamless sleep that never came, superstitious that if I were awake long enough, I would witness the earth split beneath me and the entirety of the employee lodgings plummeting into one of those wicked holes of Ashdale Mound. Still, my fascination with the place, and, yes, even those night-plaguing holes, begged my stay.

Each time I inevitably gave up on my slumber, I would walk the halls of the museum, stopping at every display, eager and careful to examine their contents. These treasured artifacts excited a primal fear and hunger in me, raising my pulse and quickening my breath. One display contained a collection of small wings, black as moonless night and soft as fresh entrails, with bone the color of ruby. Another had a large skull almost five feet in length, whose eyes had never deteriorated after death and would swivel to follow me as I passed by. My favorite was an item I had retrieved myself during my time in the society, an orb made of some undiscernible sticky substance that glowed an eerie green with a purple, formless pit in the center, forever swirling and shifting shape, holding itself in suspension about a foot above its resting place. It was on one of these rounds that immense horror rattled me to near-lunacy for a second time.

It happened during my third month at the museum. I was walking those halls riddled with monstrous curiosities when I thought I heard a peculiar buzz far off in the distance. It could not have been an insect because the pitch was unnaturally low. My first response was to ignore it. Ashdale Mound had proven itself a home to all things weird and unaccountable. Surely this was but one more oddity I could bear. But this was not to be the case. The buzzing gradually became a rumble, causing the ground to tremble beneath me. The sound further grew into a roar, until the world around me was solid noise. Staggering against the nearest display, I clutched my ears so tightly that it is a wonder I did not damage my skull.

When the land finally lay dormant once more, I had to take time to wrestle control of myself, my chest spasming and convulsing in apex panic. I did not even realize my eyes had been closed until I opened them again.

Many of the displays had fallen over. In some instances, the glass casings had shattered. Even amid my terror of the shakes, I found this quite unsettling. Something in me knew for certain that, with their displays opened, many of the contents would take on new life.

After a moment of respite, I checked my watch. Only a few minutes had passed since those violent tremors of the earth had reduced me to an effigy of unease. They felt like several lifetimes. At last composed, I made my way outside the museum to gaze on what I was sure must be great destruction to the surrounding forest.

Nothing could have prepared me for the sight that stretched before me, nor the *scope* of it. Something, to be sure, had happened to the forest, but to call it destruction would be a gross mislabeling. A vast disappearance. The earth was barren almost to the horizon. The only trees in view were off in the distance on the surrounding mountains, where dark green patches could be seen under the starlight. Before me though, a wasteland stretched out to the highway where I had left my car months ago, now a black speck in the night.

Where the trees once stood, all was barren. At least, save those damnable holes. The earth had surrounded the museum with an unending army of festering, abominable pits. That cosmos-infused soil I had seen the first night now supplanted any remnants of natural earth. I felt excitement bubble up. Not the kind experienced during my nightly walks, but one brought on by my fear and lack of comprehension for the desolation in front of me. It left me mewling and sobbing with increasing delirium until all sound from me became one long, screaming wail of despair—until something far louder and more malefic stopped me cold.

A vicious, infernal noise rose from every earthen hole at once, like a pipe organ with all its keys played together. Its beastly timbre was unlike any other, somewhere between a roar and a squeal. Perhaps that was the start of true madness. Whatever the truth of it, I awoke the next morning for the second time in front of that baneful, alluring museum, rising like a corpse. The stone steps were streaked with bloody smears, my fingernails similarly streaked and now attached to the stone, ripped from my fingertips, I suppose, as the consequence of some unconscious attempt to burrow away, claw-like, from the hellish bellowing of Ashdale Mound.

*   *   *   *   *   *

Something like tinnitus permeated my life after that night. Awake or asleep, it did not matter. Every moment of every day, I carried the blasphemous tone I had heard in my ears.

The damage to my hands deterred activity around the museum and, scared now of what had become my reality, I spent most of my time in bed, willing myself to sleep.

With each day that passed, I felt myself grow more anxious. I had been alone since my arrival, and I believed that everyone who had ever looked after the artifacts preserved here had experienced a similar sense of isolation. But circumstances had changed. I knew I needed to leave. Everyone who came before me had access to a set of magic glyph stones used for the singular purpose of creating items to keep the museum self-sufficient, a relic left behind by our society's first generation of eldritch scholars. But these had cracked during the quake and were now useless. Without the ability to summon whatever I needed, food in the museum's cold storage was reaching its end and the museum itself was in a critical state of disrepair. Not that I needed further encouragement to flee, for my fascination for that crypt of monsters had vanished entirely. Ashdale Mound was now a place that brought me only anxiety and night-mares. I had neglected to inventory the items on display after the night of the great roaring of the mound. Out of fear of what I would discover. I still held the belief that, with the breaking of the glass that undoubtedly kept their evil at bay, demonic life must have returned to many of those cursed bones and relics.

After another week of gnawing fear, I resolved myself to leave Ashdale Mound and return to New York. The food supply had run dry and I was emaciated from not having eaten in four days. Like a cornered animal, I accepted I had gone mad. I was just as mad to leave the museum as I was to have come in the first place. Something was living in the mountains here, and I was leaving the potential safety of this terrifying haven atop the mound to walk right towards it.

I packed light, only grabbing my keys to the vehicle I abandoned by the highway so long ago in what now felt like a dream. I could not allow unnecessary possessions to encumber my descent, since I knew I may be running for my life. I grasped those keys tight as I slept, ready to flee at a moment's notice. My plan was to leave at the first light of day. Even with the trees gone, navigating the holes would cause my trek back to the highway to last all day. Better to walk under the protective light of the sun for as long as possible.

I set an alarm on my phone before turning in. As I drifted off, I thought I felt a faint rumbling and heard the distant sound of a squealing roar. The sound had never left my mind in the weeks since first hearing it, though, so I convinced myself it was just another bout of madness seeing me off to sleep. I should have believed my senses then. Had I known the

consequences of that rumbling, I would have
fled Ashdale Mound that night.

*   *   *   *   *   *

My hunger weakened me in body and mind.
I have never known a more significant dread
than what I felt the next day, awakening late
to discover I had slept through my alarm. I left
the museum, cautious now because I had lost
the daylight, but still desperate to leave for the
highway. Outside, the forest had returned to
the mound and was as unnaturally verdant as
the day I had arrived. What's more, something
about the surrounding mountains in the distance
seemed different. Whether it was their form or,
perhaps, their placement, I could not say, but
their view from the steps of the museum was
disturbingly wrong. I shuddered as I recalled
the wasteland that had been there less than two
weeks ago, with its unending pox of holes. My
sanity has never recovered from that sight, and,
in fact, to this day, I continue to struggle with
differentiating dreams from memories.

Progress was slow in my descent of Ashdale
Mound. The holes were gone, but the dense plant
life was determined to snatch and claw at me
every step of the way, making my journey going
down the slope almost harder than its ascent. I
was well into the moonless night when I reached
the base of the mound. My excruciating hunger

and exhaustion, coupled with the lack of light, hampered my ability to relish any progress made. My mind whispered grim knowledge to me that, despite my best efforts, I would die in this forest. Understanding that if I continued further without rest or resources I may not rise again should I collapse, I forced myself to stop and wait, to press on the following day, and so quickly fell into dreamless oblivion.

Morning came soundlessly. No birds twittered and no wind rustled the leaves of the trees. With great effort, I awoke and rose to begin travelling again in the direction I thought I had been heading the day before. It was only about half an hour later when I stopped, again realizing my limits would be reached sooner with the summer heat dancing with my hunger. The holes were gone. Ashdale Mound and its ghoulish museum were far off in the distance now. Perhaps I was finally safe. Whatever roared that night amid the mountains could be long gone. I prayed that this was true. To survive the journey to the highway, it was imperative that I travel at night, out of the heat of the sun. With a haggard grimace, I sank back to the ground and slept the rest of the day, summoning strength for the hard, sightless trek that awaited me.

For the next three nights, I pushed forward through those harrowing woods, going to sleep each sunrise believing I would not wake up.

I do not know if that time spent got me any
closer to my destination. My sense of direction
was perpetually second-guessed by the sense
this forest was not the one I had fought through
when I first arrived there those mere three
months prior. All I know for sure is what I saw
on the fourth night. It is that death-dark night
which haunts me most; the night that the hidden
truths of the world, the grave secrets of our
reality were revealed me. I know what created
the holes on Ashdale Mound.

*   *   *   *   *   *

I do not know how long I was travelling
when it happened. Hours blurred together in
a way that seemed to bend the nature of time.
The moon had returned, now a fragile sliver
in the sky, somehow shining so that the stars
were transposed onto that otherworldly soil,
the ground faintly twinkling beneath my feet.
Shuffling along that enchanting ground, my foot
caught a vine.

As I hit the ground, tremors of unimaginable
scale began. Rumblings so violent as to knock
even the ability of thought out of one's mind. My
own mind stayed blank as the world trembled,
shifted, and crumbled around me. If I had not
fallen first, I know my body would have broken
upon the tossing, tumultuous earth. With painful
slowness, the quakes retreated enough to allow

my conscious to seep back into me. I wish that
madness had completed its embrace, that I had
finally obtained the superhuman power to shut
out this black horror, because what I saw then
was the epitome of evil: ancient, malevolent,
and insurmountable.

Around me, holes had appeared where the
trees had stood. The wastes around Ashdale
Mound had returned, allowing clear sight
to the great calamity at play; some celestial
monstrosity that had embedded itself in the
cosmic dust as our Earth was born around it.
The holes converged with the trees no more
than a few miles away from where I lay. Except
they weren't trees at all, they were fleshy things,
twisting, writhing, and churning in the most
grotesque fashion imaginable. They were slith-
ering in and out of the earth, creating the holes
that had tormented my dreams for so long.
And then it came. That hideous, blasphemous,
primordial roar that defied rationality with
pitches and frequencies designed by something
other and far greater than God.

As I looked on, my body pressed to the
ground by the unceasing tremors, the bark from
the trees in the distance fell away, ascending
like a locust plague and flitting away into the
vile, black sky. Left in their place: living pillars
shimmering with obsidian light, having stolen
the light from the stars. Fear, hunger, and
exhaustion finally overtook me and I sank into

comatose. But in my final conscious moments, I understood why I had become so lost in the forest as I glimpsed mountains in the distance sinking and the ground beneath me rising.

*   *   *   *   *   *

My next memory is of waking in a hospital. Two hunters had found me collapsed in the forest at some unknown point and brought me there. I never met them. I was several days in a coma, during which I had been nourished and hydrated with tubes and machines. I wish I could have warned the hunters. To stay away from that forest. Or any forest. I overheard the other patients in my room had become disturbed by my mutterings while I slept and I had been moved into an unoccupied room. The doctor asked me to explain to him what had happened in the woods, but I refused to say. He would think I was insane, but I know I'm fine. *I'm* the only one who has a grip on reality. It's everyone else who is insane for trusting the world we live in so blindly.

I left the country instead of returning to New York. I live in London now, far away from Ashdale Mound. But I will never feel safe. Whether the thing I saw lived in the earth or was the earth I will hopefully never know. Now, though, when the moon is out and the stars stay hidden in the sky, I take morphine and sink myself into an otherworldly oblivion.

Chest Pains
by Lee Sloan

Martin didn't know how bad off Phoebe was. The storm had toppled the colossal tree onto their house, caving in the roof as if it were made of gingerbread, partially crushing Phoebe underneath. During the tree's entrance, an angry branch as thick as an elephant's leg mangled her right orbital socket and left her eyeball dangling like a gory pendulum from its optic nerve. Martin had only seen that much blood in movies.

Martin had dragged Phoebe from the rubble and rushed the paramedics to load her onto the stretcher. Tears burned his scruffy cheeks as he followed the ambulance to the hospital. Everything that happened after was a sweeping blur.

Now, with the diminishing sound of rain outside the large glass hospital windows, water streaking down them, Martin sat in silence. The waiting room of Clear Moorings Hospital off Braxton Road was vacuous, but cozy, with yellow-orange fluorescent lights humming a one-note song above. The whirlwind of chaos Martin experienced led up to complete stillness, where he had to sit and wait like a good boy.

A nurse padded over, causing Martin to look up with hopeful eyes. She was holding a clipboard and clicking a pen. Before she could speak, Martin posed the question that had been chewing a hole in the side of his mouth, "how is she?"

The nurse clicked her pen once more and the tight seal of her lips broke.

"Mr. Tuffney, I wish I had news for you. I know this is a bad time, but would you be able to look over these insurance forms with me?"

Martin lowered his head into his hands. Corporate America. He sighed, the warm air sweeping against his palms, then looked back up.

"Miss, I need to know how she is. Does anyone have information?" His chest burn from the words.

The nurse clicked the pen, the redundant sound made Martin flinch in annoyance. The irritating hum of the fluorescents above grew louder in his ears and formed a 70s industrial music band with the nurse's belligerent pen. She scribbled something down on the top form before replying, "sir, as soon as I know something, you will, too." She smiled and walked away on bright orange Skechers, which stood in opposition to her attitude.

"Bitch," Martin murmured. He slammed his hands onto his knees and rubbed them up and down, something he did when stressed. Looking around, he decided he couldn't wait—he needed to see Phoebe.

Martin pushed a brown tuft of hair away from his eyes and looked around the scantily decorated waiting area for the nurse.

Nowhere to be seen.

Did she go to the bathroom? He did one last sweep of the waiting room and stood. He didn't have a plan, but doing *anything* was better than just sitting.

There was only one set of double doors that led back to the rest of the hospital. Nonchalantly, Martin got a closer look and saw that they needed a passkey to release.

"Fuck," he sighed.

He wasn't sure why he was surprised. Hospitals didn't want just anyone wandering into restricted areas.

Without warning, the doors flung open—and someone appeared.

Martin saw a heavyset man adorned in a hospital gown. His body odor walloped Martin in the face like a rogue barbell. The man, whose stance suggested *get the fuck out of my way*, had a wild look in his eyes. His greasy hair fell in clumps around the sides of his face and a bulbous, crooked nose, saturated with pockmarks, leaked dribbles of snot into a scanty, yellowed mustache. On his left arm, a clear piece of skin tape held a bloodied needle in place, and from this hung a tube that looked like it was

separated from an IV bag. Before Martin could
say anything, the man's meaty hands fell upon
his slender shoulders.

"Are you a doctor?" the man yelled into
Martin's face. His tongue had a thick layer of
brown fuzz coating it, and his breath smelled
like rancid pork chops and tobacco.

Martin froze, taken aback by the man's size
and stature.

"Are you a *fucking* doctor?"

"No," Martin finally answered. He went to
say more, but the man had other plans.

A fist with more horsepower than a Ferrari
coldcocked Martin's chest, sending him into
a spinning fall. Before he landed on the cold
vinyl, Martin saw the man take off for the
reception desk, shouting his grimy head off.
Martin's chest throbbed with newfound pain.
He heard another voice, shrill and angry.
Sounded like the nurse.

Martin pulled himself to a sitting position,
clutching his chest, and listened.

"Why are you up here! Are you hurt?" the
nurse screeched.

"If you're not a goddamn doctor, then I have
no business with you, you ugly redheaded cunt!
Now, find me a goddamn doctor!"

For a moment, and only a moment, he forgot
about Phoebe—the suddenness of what was
happening and all. The man that slugged him
was obviously unstable.

"Fucker hits hard," Martin said, reaching for a handrail and pulling himself to his feet. The shouting match between the nurse and the man intensified in volume.

"Sir, please! I'll call security if you don't settle down!"

Martin was on his feet in time to see the man lunge at the woman. A hellish, banshee-like scream from deep within her ribcage ricocheted off the waiting room walls. Martin watched in disbelief as the man grasped either side of the woman's face, pulled her screaming, oval head toward his—and bit down with brown teeth into the flesh and cartilage of her nose. The man's cheek muscles flexed, the surrounding skin reddening from his full bite force, a cartoon-ishly-sized vein sprawling across the enraged valley of his crimson forehead. Too quickly, the nurse's nose was disconnected from her face with a wet snap. It sounded like someone had bitten into a crisp, briny pickle. To Martin, the crazed man did it with more ease than someone pulling away an annoying scab.

"Holy shit," Martin uttered, then covered his mouth. Didn't want to call attention to himself. He couldn't see the nurse anymore because she had fallen to the floor behind the front desk. All he saw were her legs, kicking with raw agony.

"You fucking monster! Goddamn lunatic!"

"I told ya I need a doctor! Women can't *ever* listen!" the man raged.

Not long after the man's last vehement outburst, hospital security and a few doctors rushed into the room. Martin did his best to stay out of sight while chaos ensued, and eventually heard handcuffs clicking into place.

Good. At least the crazy fuck wasn't going to be taking any other noses. The passkey-protected double doors sprung open, releasing a few more hospital staff members into the waiting area. While everyone was in a tizzy, Martin saw his opportunity.

He passed through the doors and heard them close behind him. Maybe someone back here knew what was going on with his wife, or, better yet, he could see for himself without more bitchy nurses or face-eaters.

*   *   *   *   *   *

The hallway Martin found himself in was cold and featured a glassy floor with alternating blue and purple tiles. Oxygen monitors beeped from various patient rooms and reminded Martin of Morse code, disturbing what could have been a peaceful setting. The acrid smell of cleaning chemicals imbued the air.

A nurses' station, minus the nurses, greeted him. Martin assumed they were all either with patients or in the waiting room dealing with the escaped patient. Desk phones rang off the hook; call lights glowed yellow above patient doors.

Maybe one of those call lights is Phoebe.

Martin started in the direction of one of the rooms, sneakers squeaking with anticipation. He peeked into room 132 since the door was partly open. It housed an elderly woman, translucent tubes running from her nostrils like twisting snakes and feeding into a breathing machine. Her purple-splotched hands were clasped together atop her chest. Something possessed Martin to stare for a moment. The lady, despite her condition, seemed peaceful lying there with the breathy sounds of the oxygen machine playing around her.

Martin pulled himself away and approached the next room. Through a thick glass window, he could see an obese man—sweaty stomach rolls stacking and straining against each other— vomiting into an opaque red biohazard bag. The man's elephantine body lurched forward and another surge of barf chowder battled its way up his esophagus like a rioting crowd before erupting between puke-caked lips, filling out the bag. Martin watched the man turn to the window, regurgitation dripping to the ground like dirty, viscous raindrops, and wheeze, "Are you a doctor?" Martin shook his head, gave the man a limp smile, and moved on.

The following rooms didn't contain Phoebe, but each held progressively more grisly images. One of which, and perhaps the worst: a middle-aged man riddled with MRSA: avulsed flesh ravished his arms and legs, the open sores leaking pus and exposing cream-colored fat underneath. Martin felt that some of the more aggressive wounds should be packed and covered. His throat tightened when the man rolled over in the bed, groaning in pain, and one of the open sores pried away from the taut bedsheet beneath it. The pus-coated skin clinging to the fabric forced the gash to broaden and expose more beige adipose, a fatty tissue usually meant for regulating body temperature, now exposed to the elements and beginning to swell uncontrollably.

"Poor bastard," Martin breathed, turning away. There was just one room left to check—it had to be Phoebe's.

This final room had shut curtains and a closed door. Strange, since the other rooms didn't. It *had* to be Phoebe's.

With a breath of urgency, Martin pushed open the door and peered inside.

He vomited. It just happened, and his mouth hadn't the time to properly salivate in preparation for the tidal wave of beef stew bile that soon soiled his shoes and the floor. The caustic smell burned his eyes. The retch was the result of his gut reacting before his eyes and heart.

The woman in the hospital bed before him was Phoebe, but a *different* Phoebe. This new version didn't make Martin feel the way he had when they first met—how he felt when he took her on their first date to Seamus's Green. Her smiling face as she looked into his eyes across the dinner table, which was adorned with lobster tail brushed with glistening butter, mashed potatoes topped with chives, and two wine glasses, half-filled with sparkling Lambrusco, was no longer the wallet-sized Polaroid of her he kept tucked between two ridges of his brain.

No.

This attractive memory was now replaced with a new photo that plucked away the old one and mercilessly dropped it into an industrial shredder. The new photo was not of Phoebe, but of an abhorrent thing.

The thing in the bed was alive—barely. It had yellow skin that seemed to hang off the bones like damp towels on a clothesline. Feeble fingers, tremoring, clutched a hospital blanket up and over the chest; the hands rose and fell with the rhythm of labored, raspy breathing, air sucked in and pushed out of a thin-lipped mouth.

Martin remembered that the thing in the bed was his wife.

"Phoebe … oh my God … Phoebe …" he wept. He moved closer to his beloved and picked up one of her bony hands and held it between his own.

"Phoebe…" Martin was at a loss for words. His heart drummed against the walls of his chest, threatening to break free. He felt a light squeeze in his hand and looked into Phoebe's eyes—well, one of them. A haphazardly placed bandage covered the eye that had been popped out by the wrathful tree limb. Phoebe's mouth quivered, the tired throat behind it striving to form words.

He felt her limp fingers tug, pulling his body closer to hers.

"Talk to me, baby, please ..." Martin's face was a few inches away from the sunken features of what used to be the most beautiful woman in the world. Martin blinked a tear from his eye. It rolled down his cheek and formed a dark spot on the green hospital blanket Phoebe still held onto for dear life.

"Are ..." Phoebe said, as if just saying that word was equivalent to scaling Everest.

"I'm here, baby. I'm here. What is it?"

Phoebe's remaining eye widened, revealing a bloodshot, veiny balloon.

"Are you a doctor?" she asked.

Icicles pierced Martin's veins and crept into them.

"Wha ... what?"

Phoebe, with a burst of tenacity, leaned forward—and punched Martin in the chest. The blow itself was weak, but a roaring fire of agony ignited as if napalm was slathered around his heart. A gurgle of pain scorched his lips, and his eyes met Phoebe's. She was crying—heavy, desperate tears.

The fist pulled away, then struck again, bricks of coal shoveled into the blazing fire within his chest.

Martin fell. The anguish in his chest was too much. He looked for Phoebe, but she was above him now.

Footsteps. Lots of them. Sounded like the thudding of boots.

A half-dozen men, stone-faced, labored together to remove the tree that was crushing Martin's pelvis and legs.

His eyes shuttered closed, and he felt Phoebe's fist nail his sternum once more.

"Martin! Don't leave me! Stay with me! Martin!" She wiped a layer of vomit from his lips.

More footsteps. People huddled around the dying man and his desperate wife.

"Please," Phoebe begged. "Are any of you doctors?"She struck Martin's chest again, looked up, and screamed the words over and over at each person with despairing eyes.

"Are you a *fucking* doctor!"

Photo of an Animal
by Adian Suvic

"Can you take a photo of me?" I remember asking my dad. This was back when I was small enough to be whisked up and put on his shoulders. As he'd walk, I'd pluck brittle leaves from branches and collect them until they spilled out my arms. Then I'd whoosh the leaves up in the air and watch them scatter down like confetti from a parade.

His reply used to always be the same, whether it be asking for a picture or asking for another scoop of cookie dough ice cream: a smile stopping just after the canines. I always thought these would be the most unforgettable memories I'd have of him.

My dad's job was to take pictures of pets. Mondays through Thursdays, he'd set up in a studio the size of an underutilized school classroom, mount a camera on a tripod, adjust the focus, and dim orange lights. Fridays through Sundays, he'd do the same thing, only traveling to dog shows instead of his studio.

He hated animals. They made him cough and itch. His eyes watered and felt like "little hornets stinging into his irises." The dogs yammered at him as he dangled a treat from fishing wire over the lens hood. Once the yapping dogs' owners arrived, they'd stop, put away their fangs into a suitcase for the day, and return to being mommy's "treasured cupcake."

A paycheck was a paycheck, a bill was a bill, and dad was a go-getter. Through prickled eyes and slobber, he would be there. He'd smile and snap the picture. Then he left.

Years later, Mom told me to clean out his desk at his studio.

My dad saved everything.

1. Mom's recipe for chocolate chip pancakes.

2. A polaroid of the clown doll from *Poltergeist*.

3. A polaroid of my seven-year-old face crying because of the clown doll from *Poltergeist*.

4. His flaking journal from a documentary class he took in college where he'd met mom.

5. Two cheesy sonnets he wrote to mom.

6. A company calendar of the best dog photos employees took each month (dad didn't make the cut).

There was even a small manilla envelope stuffed with a lifetime's worth of tacks, staples, and paperclips packed at the bottom of the drawer. The envelope felt coarse as my hands caressed the edges. I tossed the envelope to the other side of the room. There was no use in still trying to hold something together.

I didn't want to see those memories my dad made. If he wanted them, he could've come back. He never did. He hid somewhere, away from us. They were his memories, his trinkets of the past—the same way I had memories with him. In a way, I want my kids to feel the same for me—to have those memories and think back with emotions. It doesn't have to be a smile, or a stifled laugh, or a memory that makes the skin move. But it has to be an emotion. Any. As long as there is something to attach like a dog treat on a hook.

Mom said those memories didn't matter. Because he left. He was the one to make them and walk out on them. That's what she said. Then she told me to clean his desk at the studio.

There was a shredder in the corner of his studio. Its teeth were rusted and filed; the canines missing. I unplugged it and yanked off the head. White and brown polaroid scraps snowstormed out onto the carpet.

I couldn't make out the animal from the scraps. Maybe it wasn't even an animal. Maybe it was one of us. Its face stretched and morphed as I took the white and brown scraps and jigsawed it together. Nothing seemed right. No matter how many pieces I put together, the thing wasn't defined enough. What could be

eyes stretched too far down. A tongue dragged
its way to a blue floor, or maybe a ceiling.
A rogue leg could fit perfectly in every limb
socket.

I thought about counting the scraps, but
there were piles and piles. Whatever it was, I
wanted to know why I couldn't figure it out.
How many limbs did it have? How did it walk?
How far did the fur go? Was it even fur? Was it
hair? Was that a snout? Were the rows of white
specks teeth?

Its features reminded me of a cryptid. The
white "teeth" like the shimmering wings of
Mothman and the spindly limbs like that of a
Wendigo. The holes, on what I could imagine as
missing body parts, reminded me of something
else. It was something from indigenous folklore:
a creature with gibbering countless mouths.
That's what those holes reminded me of. That's
the only thing I could make out.

The sun had fallen now and the rain would
start soon. I had to go; I couldn't stay in the
studio all night trying to decipher the shredder's
puzzle. Maybe mom was worried about me. I
put on my red raincoat and headed for the door.

Outside the studio, there was a moment
of silence. I could see black, towering clouds
against the fickle moonlight. The storm was
pulling in the wind. Rain plopped down one,
two drops at first, then it all slapped against the
studio walls. Water coursed down into storm

drains. I just stared out of those giant floor-to-ceiling windows.

I'll wait here. Mom won't care. Why would she call? *Another one left*, she'd think.

Glass exploded in the other room, jolting me back from the door. The rain and wind howled from my dad's office. I ran back to the room. The scraps scattered and blew around. They stuck to the walls, the desk, the manila envelope, the floor, the ceiling–everywhere. And I saw them. There were more mouths now. Hundreds of mouths in the scraps. Some with gnarled teeth like tree roots deep in a forest. Some with black, cancerous gums. Some with dark, inky blood. Some with bruised, victimized lips. Some showed too many teeth on one side of the face. Some like a mauled crocodile, whimpering, forced against the shoreline.

The mouths stared in my direction. I could feel them. The people these mouths belonged to–at one point in their lives–ate, spoke, laughed, communicated, shared secrets, expressed themselves. Lived. I couldn't stand them frozen in place–in the middle of a conversation. They took for granted what I didn't have.

I ran out into the storm, raincoat flapping in the wind. Something was howling from inside of the studio, behind me. Maybe it was just the rain. Maybe it was all the scraps as they gibbered, tongues getting in the way of teeth.

After all of it, the only thing I could think of as the rain cracked against me was back when I asked my dad: "Can you take a photo of me?"

In the Mist
by Aaron Joiner

As she ran through the bubbling mire, the opaque sky slithered and shimmered like wet jade overhead. The thing in the mist lay like silk over her conscious. "Come, child," it hissed with ravenous desire into her lurid mind, its every word like bloody neon dripping down her sight. Thick steps squelched in the endless abyss. It was gradual, but she was sinking. Where was there to go? *Nowhere.* The word draped over her vison and stained her mind.

The eyes in the mist were not those of evil. Evil was human. Evil was her. The eyes gleamed with patience. With understanding. With pride. With envy. She could run forever and she would only ever be in the mist, always on the precipice of absolution and humanity. Still, the girl waded on, even as the muck of her own anxiety had reached her knees.

The voice in the mist whispered, "Give yourself to me." The air vibrated around the girl with each word, as if frenzied wasps had been sown under her skin and were bursting free. The voice knew the secret truth of the world: an act of malice must be sublimated to be forgiven. But no one could forgive what she had done. "I can," it crooned, its tendrils snaking out to caress her back. The girl's strength was waning. Each step forward was through drying cement. The undulating, iridescent sky was coiling around itself. This world was shrinking, focusing itself on the voice. On her.

"You've spilled blood," cackled the hunger in the mist. "Your guilt and fear have become too heavy. Look how you sink in this bog of dreams." The girl was exhausted. The mist was now hers, coalescing her as if a familiar cloak. She felt a sultry warmth writhing around her as a rapid calm settled in. "And now I've caught you," it purred. She felt her terror trans-muting into something more welcome, a sinister adoration of sorts, longing for this reptilian unknown.

"To devour is to become," continued the friend in the mist. The girl's vision was blotted now by its drooling promises. "Be swallowed and I will forever be your guardian. Dear sinner, enter. Unburden yourself." The girl had ceased struggling, a gremlin smirk now haunting her face.

"Of course," she said, turning to face herself in the mist. The tendrils were gone. The swamp had drained, terraformed into an endless pool of blackness. The sky was crashing upon her, but with the speed and comfort of a weighted blanket. She couldn't stop herself from giggling in the dark. After all, her absolution had arrived. Reaching out with the last of her strength, the girl embraced her madness.

Savannah Abernathy's New Truck
by Lee Sloan

"Damned piece of shit!"

Savannah Abernathy of just outside Gumlog, Georgia, maybe half a mile up on Seven Forks Road, smacked a wrinkled palm over the hood of her 1987 light-blue Chevrolet Blazer. She'd had the piece of shit since it was new. Picked it up a few days after it rolled off the assembly line, spick and span, its interior permeated with that luscious new car smell.

The thing wouldn't start, again, and Savannah was running late for what she deemed a damn good sale down at the Calico Country Store.

The tired old woman ran yellowing finger-nails through wispy gray hair, a knot of it catching on one of her rings and tugging her scalp, only angering her more.

"Hell with it!" the irritated senior citizen shouted to the muggy Georgia sky. She kicked one of the front tires, varicose veins gleaming under sweltering sunshine.

A hand gnarled from the plagues of arthritis pulled an oversized phone—one of those cell phones made for old and visually impaired

people with extra-large buttons–from the pocket
of her tattered yellow muumuu. She turned
her hunched back to the sunlight, trying to
see the phone screen better. A crippled finger
scrolled through a list of contacts, stopping on
one Miss Cherry Hollis. Savannah and Cherry
were lifelong friends, but Savannah couldn't
remember Cherry's phone number if her life
depended on it.

Savannah smashed a bitter finger onto the
call button and pressed the phone against an
ear adorned with one simple flower earring. She
scratched just below a cutaneous horn housed
behind her ear on the opposite side of her head.
The horn, which she refused to have removed
because she hated doctors, had been with her
almost as long as the Blazer.

The phone rang a few times, and a scratchy
voice answered, "Hello?" Cherry sounded
like she was stirring from the effects of a long
afternoon nap; she loved those.

"Cherr, I need a ride down to Albert's. The
Blazer's down for the count and I need to make
the sale going on. Wallet's stretched thin."

Albert was the owner of the Calico Country
Store. Savannah referred to the store by Albert's
name and had done so since he opened in 1997.

Silence on the other end of the phone.

Savannah tapped her foot, then hollered into
the jumbo phone, "Yoo-hoo! Cherry! You fall
asleep on me?"

Cherry cleared her throat through the reception static. "Fine. Give me a bit to get ready."

The call ended before Savannah could reply, something Cherry did when she was annoyed. Savannah knew this, but didn't care. She needed those damned groceries.

Putting the phone back into the muumuu pocket, Savannah gave the Blazer one more good whack on its semi-rusted hood and rushed into her double wide. She wanted to change into the proper shoes before going out.

In no time, Savannah heard Cherry rapping on the front door of the trailer.

"Hold yer horses, I'm coming!" Savannah shouted, scooping her keys from a wicker table adjacent to her recliner. The recliner, like the Blazer, was on its last leg. Savannah had worn a molding of her body into the chair, and the armrests were flat as pancakes, no padding inside to comfort her gaunt arms.

Savannah locked the front door and hurried to Cherry's cream-colored Plymouth sedan; Cherry was already back inside it, stooped over the steering wheel, one of those scented trees almost touching the top of her head. Cherry was even smaller in frame than Savannah, and quite a few years older. Albeit the two of them bickered daily, there existed an inseparable bond between them, fostered through years of holidays, family gatherings, family deaths,

vacations, cry sessions, and joyous moments —
age just made them both a bit rough around the
edges.

Savannah pulled herself into the passenger
seat, a purse zipper rubbing noisily against the
snakeskin material of her trusty handbag.

Cherry craned her neck toward Savannah.
"Do you really have to bring that enormous tote
with you everywhere?"

Savannah huffed, unzipping and digging
around in the bag. "Oh, shut up, Cherry, you
always have something to say. Are you taking
me or not?"

Cherry snorted and turned away, shifting
the car into drive and maneuvering the two of
them out onto the dirt road that led to town.

Tinny Christian music leaked through
old car speakers. The two of them listened in
silence for a few minutes — well, almost silence;
Savannah continued rustling about in her purse,
much to the annoyance of Cherry.

The sedan bounced along a rough stretch of
road that weaved through a thick expanse of
Georgia pine and then turned on to Holcomb
Drive. A young couple was coming out of
Albert's as Cherry pulled up. She waved them
along and then pulled up as close as she could
to the two yellow pylons that protected the
entrance. Savannah fished a faded wallet from
the purse, then placed the purse on the floor
between her legs. Cherry took note of this.

"So, you bring that heaping bag, only to bring the damn wallet inside?"

Savannah tossed her arms into the air, the wallet in hand rubbing against the upholstery. "See, there you go again! Always running that fat mouth of yours."

Cherry stuck out her tongue at Savannah and went to cut the engine, her hand hitting the wiper lever and triggering the wiper blade to glide across the window with a dry squeal, a waving arm welcoming them to Albert's.

"See, look what ya did. You're gonna wear out those wipers treating them like that," Savannah scoffed, pushing the passenger door open.

"It was an accident, you ninny," Cherry retorted, pulling the key from the ignition and unbuckling her seatbelt.

The two of them headed towards the glass door entrance, a single door like the side door of any farmhouse, when Cherry grabbed Savannah's arm.

"Vann, look! Right over there!"

Savannah peered across the crushed gravel parking lot in the direction Cherry was pointing and saw a petite brown pickup truck with a bright red FOR SALE sign crookedly plastered to its rear window.

Cherry slapped Savannah in the arm. "That's exactly what you need! Can get rid of that old piece of shit and stop bugging me!"

A smile broke across Cherry's face, pulling her deeply etched cheek wrinkles taut around her mouth.

"Hell, Cherr, I can't afford a new truck! Why do you think I'm here for this dag-blasted sale?"

Cherry scowled. "I know you're hoarding a little fortune up in that trailer of yours. Time to dig into your other wallet, Vann."

Savannah tightened her lips. She wouldn't admit it, but she knew Cherr was right. She needed a new truck.

"Oh, I'll have a look at it after we shop. Can't waste another minute and risk losing all the good stuff from the sale."

Inside, a young redheaded boy greeted them from a register. He was ringing up groceries for a middle-aged couple that looked like they hated each other.

Savannah ignored the boy and grabbed a shopping basket from the rack near the entrance and headed to the produce section and the first of the sale signs. Albert's always put her favorites on sale, or so she thought. Meanwhile, Cherry stood near the register and flipped through a few of the used car flyers.

A moment later, Savannah appeared next to Cherry, several grocery bags hanging from her arms, the thin plastic pulling on decrepit skin, purpling it.

"Okay, Cherr, got what I needed. You didn't get anything?"

"You know I don't go crazy for these sales like you do. Listen, I flipped through all these here flyers, and not one of the price tags look worth what's in the picture. You better give that truck outside a chance. Could be your new best thing."

Savannah tuned out the first part of what Cherry said. She had learned over the years that when listening to Cherry, it was usually the end of the sentence that contained the point of the whole damn thing.

"If it'll shut you up, I'll see if there's a number on the sticker to call."

Cherry smiled, a flash of silver molar fillings revealed.

"Smart girl. Load up your hoard, first."

The two elderly friends left Albert's and Cherry popped her trunk, allowing Savannah to deposit a lifetime's worth of groceries.

"Shit, Vann, did you leave anything for anyone else?" Cherry frowned and huffed, slamming the trunk.

"Get off my ass, Cherr. I won't have to shop again for a while, which means I won't need you and your attitude to pick me up!"

"In that case, go back in and buy what's left so we can extend the deal!"

Cherry laughed and nudged her friend's shoulder, causing Savannah to crack into a smile. She turned to face the truck; it was patiently waiting right where they left it.

"See, right there," Cherry pointed. Below the FOR SALE sign was a sun-faded phone number. Savannah went through the arduous task of retrieving her cell phone and punching in the number. It took a few tries because her finger kept hitting 4 instead of 5.

She got it. Savannah pressed the phone to her ear, her other hand protecting her eyes from the relentless sunlight.

A click, then a tired voice fizzled into existence over the line.

"Hello?"

"Uh, yeah, hi there. I'm calling about the truck for sale. Saw it parked here near Albert's."

The throat on the other end of the line cleared and sheets rustled. Sounded like the guy had been asleep and was rolling over in bed.

"Near Albert's?"

"Uh, yeah, I mean, uh, Calico's. You know."

"Sure, sure," the voice cracked. "Were you interested in it?"

"Well, that depends on the price, and if there is anything wrong with her," Savannah said, watching Cherry pop open a pill bottle and dump an Advil into her palm.

"Nope, not a thing wrong with her. She needs oil a bit more often than most, but that's normal for those kinds of trucks. Cold air and radio, though," the man piped up.

Silence. Savannah bit her lip. So far, it sounded like a damn good truck.

"All right. How much are you asking for it?"

Silence, this time on the man's end.

Savannah looked at Cherry, who was swishing water around in her mouth.

"I can let her go for two," the man replied.

"Two thousand?" Savannah hollered into the phone.

"Yes, ma'am. That outside your price range?"

Savannah almost choked on air. "No! No! That's not a bad deal at all for a used truck these days, especially with air and tunes."

"Excellent!" the man said. "Would you like to meet up, say, tomorrow at Albert's?"

Savannah cocked her head. "Any chance we could just get it over with? My friend is my chauffeur today. I think she's ready to kill me."

The man laughed.

"I suppose that's possible. Give me an hour and I can meet ya there with the keys and the title. Sound good to you?"

"Yes, I mean it sounds good."

"My name's Frank, by the way."

"Yes, Frank ... my name's Savannah. Thank you."

The call ended and Savannah went over to Cherry to celebrate, but Cherry was already doing a little celebratory dance.

"Oh, stop it!" Savannah barked. "Get me home, quick, so I can grab the money."

"With pleasure!" Cherry said, shuffling to the driver's side door of her car.

The two of them headed back to Savannah's trailer. Cherry was driving a little faster than usual.

*   *   *   *   *   *

After Savannah put away all the new groceries, she scuttled to her bedroom and began rummaging through a coffee can perched on the top shelf of a walk-in closet. The can had a little over three grand in hundreds and fifties in it. Her rainy-day fund. The coffee can had developed a thin layer of rust around it—the last rainy day involved a new roof for the trailer after a tree fell on it during an aggressive thunderstorm. Savannah was lucky it was just the roof; some poor woman down the road saw her husband crushed under a tree from the same storm.

She gathered and counted two thousand dollars, then placed it into an envelope which was sealed with her spit and one piece of clear tape. She walked up to her bathroom door and banged on it.

"Cherr, hurry up! I don't want to miss this man because you're taking your sweet time in there!"

"Hold yer damn horses! My back's spasming!"

Savannah banged her first on the door, harder. "Lord have mercy, Cherr!"

After a few more minutes, Savannah heard the toilet flushing and Cherry pulling her pants up, followed by the squeak of the sink handle. Savannah sighed and leaned her forehead against the cold wood of the door.

"You're gonna need Jesus if you don't hurry the hell up!" Savannah shouted through an age-creased mouth.

The door opened and Cherry appeared.

"Let's go, you goon," she huffed, and moved for the front door.

*   *   *   *   *   *

On the way back to Albert's, Savannah opened the envelope and counted the money three more times.

"It's all there, Vann," Cherry griped, flicking on her blinker.

"You just focus on driving," Savannah snipped, counting the money a fourth time.

Cherry parked in the same spot as before. The sky had started to cloud over. Looked like rain. *The perfect day to tap into her rainy-day fund*, she thought. She looked at the envelope with the money a moment and then at her friend and then over at the truck. Nobody. She pulled her phone out, ready to call Frank, when the front door of Albert's opened. Someone with swept back gray hair walked out, holding a Slim Jim in one hand and a Coke Zero in the other. The middle-aged man approached the truck and leaned against the hood. Savannah watched him crack open the soda can and guzzle half of it before peeling away the plastic of the Slim Jim and chomping off a good third of it.

Savannah slipped out of Cherry's Plymouth and approached the truck. The man did not seem to notice.

"Sir, are you Frank? I spoke with you about the truck?"

"Haven't talked ta anyone else today about it," the man said, setting the can down on the hood of the truck and pocketing the Slim Jim.

"Glad to meet ya," he said, extending his hand.

"Likewise."

Savannah shook the man's hand and could feel his callouses.

"Mind if I give it a quick test drive?"

Savannah looked back at the Plymouth, at Cherry, as if to ask for approval.

Cherry lit a cigarette.

"Sure thing."

Frank placed a silver key into Savannah's palm and she laughed.

"Trust me not to steal it?"

A flash of sunlight broke through the cloudy sky and ricocheted off Frank's eyes.

"I trust ya," he said and smiled.

Savannah gave a nod and invited Cherry to ride with her. She unlocked the driver's side door of the truck. She opened the door and looked inside. Clean. Even smelled nice. She pulled herself into the seat and closed the door, then reached over and unlocked the passenger side for Cherry, who climbed in. The truck rocked in response. Savannah stared through the windshield at Frank. He kept smiling. Something about it made her uncomfortable, but this feeling was subdued by the truck's engine roaring to life after she started it. Sounded good. She maneuvered the truck onto Holcomb Drive, the crushed gravel dusting up behind her as she left the parking lot. Felt good so far.

"Oh! Music!" Savannah remembered. She twisted the radio knob to ON and heard a crisp guitar riff fill the cab. Savannah clapped in delight. She adjusted another dial and felt cold air sweep over her lined face.

"Air and radio, yes, sir!" she cried, tapping the top of the steering wheel in approval. Cherry was busy nodding her head along to the music.

Savannah did a U-turn somewhere along U. S. 17 and brought the truck back to Albert's, listening to the guitar solo of "Free Bird" complete with ice cold air conditioning.

*　　　*　　　*　　　*　　　*　　　*

By the time Savannah got back, the threat of rain had passed and the Georgia sun was shining hot and fierce. Frank was still smiling— skintight and thin-lipped.

"Well, whadda ya think?"

He downed the last swig of cola and tossed the can into a trash bin.

"She's a beauty. I'll take her," Savannah said, trying to sound serious and business-like, but joy pressed up through her throat and made her voice shaky.

"Great! Can get ya the truck and the title today, and we can arrange to have it officially put into your name later this week. How's that sound?"

"That'll be just fine!" Savannah beamed, her coffee-stained dentures now seeming white in the sunlight. After a few moments of casual conversation, the truck was Savannah's. Frank took the money, counted it, and deposited the title into Savannah's hand. She took down his name and number and they agreed to meet later that week at the Tag Office in Carnesville to complete all the legal mumbo jumbo.

A moment later, Frank got into his car, a modest two-door coupe, and drove away, leaving Savannah boasting with pride over her new baby.

"Can you believe it, Cherr? She's all mine! She's wonderful!"

"What I can't believe is that I don't have to be your personal taxi company anymore, thank you very much!"

Cherry gulped back a laugh as Savannah embraced her in a hug.

"Thanks for driving me around, Cherr. I know it's been hard on you."

Cherry returned the hug.

"You know I have no choice but to put up with you, Vann," she said in a warm voice. "But I'm gonna head home now. My soap is starting soon. Don't drive like the mad woman you are, Vann. I need you to get home in one piece."

Cherry pulled out of Albert's parking lot for the second time that day and Savannah got into her new truck. She sat quietly for a moment, admiring the simple interior. Then without thinking, she turned the key and the engine purred to life, just as it had done before. Cold air kicked on and greeted her.

"I think I'll call you Buster," Savannah said. She patted the dash, then drove home with Warren Zevon's "Lawyers, Guns and Money" caressing her ears and the beautiful A/C cooling her head and providing respite from the unforgiving Georgia sun.

*   *   *   *   *   *

Savannah parked Buster next to her old truck. "Out with the old, in with the new!" she told her Blazer and smacked its hood.

Inside, Savannah made a cup of hot chamomile tea, something she did most nights to help her get settled. She fidgeted between the armrest and cushion of her recliner, trying to find the remote control, when a knock sounded at the front door.

"Ugh! It's late! Who on earth is that?" Savannah asked herself, pushing the leg rest back into the chair and standing. She pushed an eye against the peephole and saw that it was Cherry.

Savannah unlatched the door and opened it.

"Cherr, what's going on? Everything okay? It's late."

"Vann, can I come in? Something happened."

Savannah's face dropped. She ushered her friend inside and closed the door, relatching it. Savannah made a spot for Cherry on the couch and the two of them sat down next to each other.

"Cherr, what happened? You're scaring me."

Cherry looked at the ground. Savannah watched her twiddle her thumbs together.

"I think there's something wrong with your new truck, Savannah," Cherry said, her voice trembling like static.

"What do you mean? It drives just fine. I test drove it and ..."

"No. You need to look outside, Savannah. Look at the truck."

Savannah felt dread wash over her. She was a rigid old woman, but something about the way Cherry spoke had caused a sudden thickening in her blood. What could be wrong with the truck?

Savannah stood up from the couch and walked hesitantly to the front window, but before she could look at the truck, the phone rang. She snatched the phone off the receiver and pressed it to her ear.

It seemed an act of desperation.

"Yes? Hello?" she asked, a concoction of trepidation and annoyance in her tone. The voice that replied on the other end of the line brought out a raw form of fear that Savannah had never experienced, and consequently, did not know how to handle. It felt like a gut punch of terror.

"Vann? It's Cherr. I think you left one of your grocery bags in my trunk."

Savannah felt warm urine drenching her underpants. The warmth spread. A radiating, terminal warmth. Still clenching the phone to her ear, she turned her head back to face Cherry on the couch, but Cherry was no longer there. In her place was some sort of thing, sitting on the couch.

"Vann? Are you there? Vann?" Cherry said through the phone speaker.

Savannah did not hear the question. She looked at the thing on the couch—watched it speak to her. Not *thing* exactly. Vaguely human. Or once was.

"Something ... wrong ... with ... the ... truck ... wrong ... with ... the ... truck," the vaguely human, once-was thing said.

Savannah dropped the phone. It banged into the wall and bounced from its cord and kept bouncing.

"Something. Wrong. With. The. Truck."

The vaguely once-was human thing craned its neck back, back, back, like a memory receding.

"Something wrong with ..." the same words now crackling out of the dangling phone.

Savannah forced herself to look out the window at the truck—and saw that it was wrecked. Destroyed.

She turned to the thing, to see its head lean back, further than any head should ever go—and watched it detach from the body and drop to the floor behind the couch.

Savannah screamed. The scream sent her voice hoarse.

Then silence.

*   *   *   *   *   *

Along U. S. 17, a half-dozen deputies assessed what the sheriff called the worst accident he had ever seen in Franklin County. Two elderly women, one of them decapitated in the accident, were identified as Savannah Abernathy and Cherry Hollis.

"Damn shame," Sheriff Tennen whispered. He was holding a photo from Savannah's wallet. The picture showed her seated at a breakfast table with Cherry. Looked like it was twenty years prior.

A few miles back at Albert's, Frank was dialing the sheriff's office to report that his truck had been stolen.

It Comes Back

by Adian Suvic

I've been having weird dreams—ones that
I don't think are mine. I don't know why they
came to me, but they did. Dreams of blood,
violence. Once, twice, maybe three times a
week. They came back no matter what, and I
need them to stop.

Because of the dreams, I bit down on my
pillow. Every single night, my dull teeth sank
into the memory foam. I first learned it from my
wife, Alina. Sometimes, it'd be her pillow, with
a curved row of small rectangles around the
corner. Every time it happened, she'd horse-kick
me awake. It truly didn't matter if I bit into my
pillow or my wife's; my bite had no bias. Some
nights, I woke up knowing what I had done,
even before my wife told me with a look, not
because of the feel of silky fabric in my mouth,
but because of the bite marks. Memory foam
will do that: it'll remember.

It gets bad enough that my wife wakes up
from the sopping, sucking sounds. Kick square
to the back. My jaw locked, but somehow,
through force, my sleeping side managed to pop
it back into place. After my wife told me about

it, she decided to sleep on the couch, just until I
see the doctor and ask what the hell is going on.

A week later, after being assaulted by those
weird dreams and retaliating on my pillows,
I nestled in Dr. Cosset's cluttered office. I sat
on a wobbly stool with no backrest, crammed
between two life-sized porcelain sheep statues. I
turned my head a couple degrees and used one
of the horns to scratch an itch behind my ear.

"Stop that," Dr. Cosset said in a nasally
voice. He was dwarfed by his desk and sheep
statues. "Now—" I didn't catch it at first, but
he elongated every O and W sound "—*weird*
dreams, you say. Monsters, mouths, and teeth
with blood? These oddities might come from an
acute line of stress." He rubbed the tuft of hair
on his chin. "I'm not your therapist; I can't tell
you or your psyche what to do. But I can make
you fall asleep. And forget just enough so you
can sleep."

If I wasn't already having weird dreams,
the look in Dr. Cosset's eyes would give me
some. He categorized it as the "not truly ill, but
close enough to make a quick buck" part of the
gig. I imagined a scoopful of little yellow pills
zigzagging their way into the bottle and me
handing over a cut of my check for them. "Take
two every night for a week, twenty minutes
before bed," Dr. Cosset said.

The night I picked up the pills, I sat on my
bed, those little yellow imaginary pills real and

in my palm. I rolled them around, watching them clink against each other. My grandfather used to talk in his sleep. Granddad Dan blabbed about anything, from all forty-two cracks in his apartment to how his side won the Vietnamese War. Grandma Maggie said he dabbled in voodoo—drawing black circles at home, staring at wild animals for a little too long, and buying more and more blocks of wax. Grandma Maggie was a fundamental Christian; she didn't like a damn thing Grandad Dan was doing. Him talking in his sleep was the end of it. One night, she took a hacksaw from the garage and yanked his old, loose lips far enough away from his face to tear into the flesh. In her history of family violence, she thought it was for the best.

Alina left for the couch downstairs, fringe pillow in arm. I licked my lips. My wife wasn't as faithful or superstitious as Grandma Maggie, but I wanted to keep my lips. I swallowed the pills, laid on my back, and stared out into the blackness. There was the hum of the air conditioning, the faint movement of my wife stirring below me, the bleakness in the back of my mind. Did we even own a hacksaw?

My brain, or something in my brain, tingled. I think it was the pills. A feeling crept up from the back to my frontal lobe. Part of me felt paralyzed. It's like I was lying in my bed for hours. I couldn't tell if I closed my eyes or if I was still just staring off into the blackness. I didn't sleep and dream, instead I remembered something.

I was on my side, in a bed I didn't own. From the corner of my eye, I saw a silhouette in the dark, on top of me. The silhouette squeezed my lips, yanking them away from me. They brought down something sharp against my lips. My skin seared. The sensation of a hacksaw with gaps in its teeth slicing through my skin burned more than my screaming throat—but I didn't make a noise. I couldn't. This wasn't my memory.

Grandad Dan laid in bed while it happened, limbs dead, unable to signal any spasm. Grandma Maggie sliced through it like a fresh tomato. The blood trickled, then coursed on the white pillows. She muttered to herself, about her faith, about the imaginary voodoo.

I stirred awake by the alarm. Alina was just now walking into my room. She had a photo-graph in her hand.

"Are you ready to look at it?" she asked.

I blinked at the question. All the heat left my body. "I don't think I'm ready yet. My dreams are getting better. I promise."

*   *   *   *   *   *

The two life-sized porcelain sheep statues looked at me as I walked past them to sit. I noticed a cartoonish face on one and a more stoic face on the other. It was like I was on trial, in front of guardians of some sacred gate; one only tells the truth, while the other tells lies. I moved the stool away from them.

Dr. Cosset grunted through the door, patient chart under his arm. "What a week, huh? Blooming or wilting?" His face held those *O* and *W* sounds again, like the groaning of an old warship. "And have you scheduled an appointment with a therapist yet?"

I rubbed my head. "I haven't had time to schedule anything yet. But my dreams are … better. Fewer bite marks this week. Though, maybe they were deeper. More powerful."

"Oh." He was almost disappointed. "Not blooming?"

"Well. Not wilting." After the night where my Grandma Maggie hacked my lips off—or Granddad Dan's lips off—I only had one other weird dream that week. Most of them were weird, but there was only one intense enough to crawl into nightmare territory. "It was different," I said. "In a better way."

"Ohh." The note of disappointment pitch-changed to something comical. "Better is good. Being simple and obvious is good. You were sleeping, correct?"

"Like a log with eyes would."

"Hmm." He smoothed out his goatee. "What were the dreams you're concerned with? The oddities?"

I told him about my dream during the first night I took the pills. I swayed from some details: the blood on the pillows, my Grandma Maggie on top of me as my Granddad Dan, the sweat, her stone face, her voodoo.

"Monstrous." Dr. Cosset opened a desk drawer, hid a hand inside, and shuffled through bottles. Pills rattled within those near-vacant bottles. "And you felt the entire thing–the entire sensation?"

"It burned, but my lips are still here." I gave a wan smile. Better than Grandad Dan and what he looked like.

Dr. Cosset took his hand from the desk and produced a small bottle, a smidgeful of yellow pills visible through it. "Nothing else," he said. "No other strange dreams?"

The other strange dream lingered. I was fishing at Johndee Lake. My fishing rod was a toy in my hands, unfamiliar and splintering. Voices cluttered around my ears. There was an older man, both muscular and smaller, more delicate than as I am now, and a young boy, faceless. The boy wore nothing but a red raincoat. He was nude underneath, yet I knew his skin was red, blistering, taut.

Something caught on the fishing rod's hook. My stomach keeled and turned inside out as if it knew what was caught. There was no way of me knowing. Was this a memory or a dream? The water gurgled under my line, dragging it down.

A disfigured snout rose out the water. It's skin peeled back, revealing the fresh, pink meat underneath. My stomach churned. The eyes were gone, replaced with flabby, puffy meat that draped out of the socket in fat mounds. It was a crocodile, or something that tried to still be one.

I kept that dream hidden to myself. The moment I'd tell Dr. Cosset that, he'd slam down a button and two burly men would hold me down to stop me from hurting myself.

"Nothing else," I told him.

Dr. Cosset played with the pill bottle in his hands, like I did just before taking them. "Starting tomorrow night, take an additional pill." He unsealed the bottle, tapped three out, and presented them to me. "Three. Like so. It seems you started counting sheep again, so I'm just making sure." He smeared his lips into a smile, bottom teeth hidden, top teeth in a row. A dead smile from a dream.

*   *   *   *   *   *

The pills slid against the walls of my throat. And there I was again, staring at the blackness above and around me. If I close my eyes, I'll sleep. Should I have told Dr. Cosset about my fishing dream? About that boy and that thing in the water? If I did, I wouldn't have to take these pills. But maybe three's the magic number:

maybe with these three, I won't have those dreams anymore. I was lying. I kept my eyes tight, waiting for another nightmare to slither up.

We sat in a car at the bank of Johndee. The older man up front, clutching the steering wheel like he did something he shouldn't have; he held it with pent up innocence and remorse. The boy in the red raincoat was next to me in the back, trying to hold in his tears, chest huffing, skin too ruddy, cracking open like scales. The doors were opened. We all faced ahead, seat belts locked in like chains, eyes vacant, forward, following the mangled crocodile as it dragged itself towards us.

Eye meat flopped down the side of the crocodile's face. Its mouth hung open as if it could talk. In attempts to drag itself, the poor thing struggled on stretches of soft sand. It tumbled, water catapulting out of its mouth.

The boy's chest ballooned up. His skin changed: the scales clasped in place, holding something back. The color drained, leaving behind a white opaqueness, like a drowned body. His chest puffed and kept growing, until the seatbelt barely held it in place. Then, it dropped. Lake water surged out of him, a torrent through his mouth, eyes, ears.

The older man kicked open the car door. There was a can in his hand. Full. Heavy. He gained on the crocodile, standing above the pathetic thing. Down it went, smashing into the creature's face, turning the sand red. "Billy. Billy! BILLY!" He hammered the can in, again and again, like crooked nails through wrists.

I flailed awake, hands twitching. Alina stared from the doorway. Her face had a look of the unknown. She had seen something in the middle of my dream. "Your mouth stretched open," she said, "like a crocodile's."

*   *   *   *   *   *

Alina showed me the photograph. I was hesitant to take it, expecting to see it talk to me, an infinite set of gibbering mouths. Her soft skin caressed my arms and hands again. "I took the picture," she said. "Not him. Your dad's not here."

Whenever I tried to look at the picture, my eyes shot in a different direction. My hands were cold against hers. I felt her fingers, how thin and precious they were. "You're not going to horse-kick me again if I don't look, right?"

She managed a tiny laugh. "No. Only if you start biting the photo."

My eyes flicked from her to some vacant spot in the room. "Heh." I inhaled, held it to three, then let it escape. I pressed her gentle fingers, then faced the photograph.

I could barely recognize Billy. His mouth was torn open. Black sludge filled it to the teeth, spilling from his blue lips. His skin was white, bloated, with bulbous pockets as if a thin bedsheet was thrown over a set of billiard balls. One eye forever cut open from the impact of the water. That's the story they told us. It was more than likely a sharp rock hidden under the water's surface.

My breathing slowed as I looked over each detail. It wasn't hard to breathe, I just stopped for a moment, taking it all in. My hand unfurled, and I noticed Alina's fingers were a yellow-white. She sat there and nodded.

I opened my mouth, but nothing came out. Inhale, hold, let go. "Am I guilty for Billy?"

"No," she said. "He was the one drinking." She really was precious.

I thought of my father. These giant glass panes were the memories he forced onto me. Any simple crack, any shard that snaps off— able to slice away at my lips, at my thoughts. "I should—" I cleared my throat. "I want to talk to him about Billy."

Ashes to Dust

by Aaron Joiner

Chattering was everywhere. It clanged in his head. It rattled his teeth. Caleb had heard that the lowest level of Hell was actually the coldest because it was furthest from God's light. He wondered if that's where he was now. His breath steamed inside the somber, dank shed. The grey, rotted wood composing the structure had taken on an ethereal hue from the morning light that was pushing through soon-to-burst clouds and grimy windows.

"Will you say a prayer with me?" a woman's voice asked from across the room as he inspected the cobwebs and black mold on the ceiling.

Rebecca was rubbing the dust off her mittens and onto her jeans, staring at him from the farthest wall of the cramped shed, where all the pictures lined the shelves. Her voice trembled as she asked, although it seemed to Caleb to be from more than the deep chill that was keeping him rooted by the doorway.

"I can't. You know that."

"You can," she replied, her voice stiff as she glared at him.

Caleb didn't respond. Instead, he turned his attention to the old toolbox. Rebecca's brother, Adrian, had repurposed it years ago on the farm into a sort of shrine. It might have been part of the ritual a long time ago, but the thick dust over it suggested that only the placing of the family pictures remained in the ceremony.

"It's for *him*. Please, Caleb." Caleb turned away from the rusted, dusty shrine and found her cradling the urn like a newborn.

"Seriously, Becky, I— "

"Goddammit, Caleb," she hissed. "Say the fucking prayer. He's your *fucking son*."

His teeth had stopped chattering. A heat was rising in Caleb amid the tightness in his chest. Behind where Rebecca stood with the urn, the shelves upon shelves of pictures with urns of their own loomed over the room, an audience to what Caleb knew would become a mistake on his part. The eyes of accusers. Was the prayer a rite of passage to join them?

"You're damn right," Caleb snapped back. "Andrew is my son, too. And yet here we are, on your brother's farm in Nowhere, Idaho, banishing him to dusty oblivion with the rest of your brood. I agreed to put him to rest with your family, despite my distaste for it. So let's skip the fucking prayer. What god condones a child's banishment into a cold crypt like this?"

"Then where would you have taken him?" Rebecca shouted, tear-stained and rancorous.

"There was no objection, *not one*, when I mentioned this place. Like a loyal dog, you came with me, no questions asked. And *now*, now that we're out here, hundreds of miles from home, *now* you speak up? He's with family here. What the fuck is your problem? Where is this place that has just now come to you, that is better than being with the family that loves him?"

"Somewhere ..." Caleb took a moment to compose himself. The bottom of his palms stung from where he'd been digging his fingernails into his skin. "Somewhere in the sun, Becky. Somewhere warm and beautiful that's maybe a little—a little representative of how much we love him. This place, and I'm sorry for saying so, but it's awful. I don't want to leave him here. This isn't his family. We are. He never knew these people and neither did you."

He turned and opened the door to the shed. A sharp breeze cut through the room, biting his face and rattling the shelves.

"Where are you going?"

"To give you space to pray."

"Please, Cay," Rebecca's voice had lost all of its passion, becoming the faintest mewling, "don't leave me to do it alone. It's little Andy ... it's our baby boy. Don't go."

Caleb turned for one last look at his disheveled, haggard wife. They'd both been through so much these past few weeks since the accident. Some nights he laid awake wondering how they could keep being a family after all this. The corners of his mouth felt tight now, and it hurt to speak.

"I can't believe that any god in any religion can hear prayers that are offered in this place. Just look at all the dust and disarray. Not even Adrian and Natalie visit. The dead are forgotten here."

He shut the door behind him and began walking down the overgrown dirt path towards the farmhouse. He imagined Natalie at the stove and Adrian seated at the kitchen table, the two of them waiting for him and Rebecca to return for fajita omelets and buttered toast with that boysenberry spread they liked to keep on hand. On his hands, he could feel the pinpricks of what was about to be a major storm. Andrew had loved the rain. It had always been a battle with him to keep mud out of the house.

There had been mud that day, too. All over the boy. Painted like tribal markings and camouflage on his face. The trucker on his knees. Mud on him, too.

I didn't see him. I didn't see him.

Caleb stopped. Still a distance away, the lights were on in the kitchen window of the farmhouse. Breakfast was almost ready. Suddenly, he broke away from the path at a run. He didn't know where he wanted to be. Just not here.

*   *   *   *   *   *

Caleb had no idea how much time had passed once he'd finally exhausted himself. It hadn't felt long, but it must have been. He was at the property line at the top of the slope where the highway ran. Chest heaving, he sat down.

The grass was soaked. The rain had become like falling teardrops for God-knows-how-long. The mud had squelched under him when he'd sat. His pants would be caked in it when he finally stood back up.

The highway was dead. Every several minutes, a car sped by pushing double the speed limit. Way out here, he supposed there was no reason not to. The blacktop itself was glistening under the dreary morning light, a serene presence in the stillness.

A fawn and its mother appeared from the dense green on the other side of the asphalt. Caleb watched them, still and quiet, as they moved tentatively along the curb. It seemed as though the child was still learning to walk, falling or stumbling every few paces. Each spill coated its fur a bit more in mud.

I wonder how exasperated the mother is.

Several silent moments passed before the mother looked his way. Could she tell he wasn't part of the scenery? Then the herding began: the great pilgrimage across the highway. It was slow going. The fawn didn't seem to want to follow and the road was slick.

After many minutes of slipping and corralling, a loud noise startled the three of them. The ground was shaking. A horn was blaring.

A truck was coming.

The driver was leaning on the horn, pleading with the deer to move.

I didn't see him.

The road was too wet. The truck was too large. And the trucker was driving even faster than the other vehicles that Caleb had seen pass. He wouldn't be able to stop in time.

The deer stood frozen; heads turned toward their impending undertaker. The horn continued to beg for their lives. The storm clouds had become like slashed arteries, bleeding out overhead.

Move.

The truck was getting too close.

Move. Please.

The truck was upon them now.

Andy, move!

"Hey!"

The deer turned, their gaze meeting Caleb's. He thought he saw a sadness in them, a resolved knowingness that they had waited too long. The truck passed, tires still screeching against the oncoming calamity. Caleb turned away at the last moment. With his eyes closed and his chest convulsing, the rain felt warm on his face.

I didn't see him.

Slowly, he opened his eyes, steeling himself for what was in front of him. He saw the deer, still staring at him. The mother had been reluctant to leave her child. Caleb was sure she would have run, otherwise. The truck was out of sight. All that remained of it now was thick skid marks on the road. Somehow, the driver had managed to change lanes at the very last moment. The child had been spared.

*   *   *   *   *   *

Chattering. Intense chattering. Caleb was bludgeoned with rain the entire walk back to the shed, an arctic chill setting into his bones. A coalition of fatigues hit him after the event on the highway. He didn't want to move anymore. Or think. Or feel. But he had to.

Whatever Natalie had made was being carried to him on the damp, sluggish wind. With luck, his breakfast would still be warm when he finally made it back to the farmhouse. He trudged, shivering, towards the faint aroma.

He was back on the dirt path, almost to the shed, when he heard a shrill scream from within. Caleb, with exigent fear, sprinted the rest of the way to the shed, burning through the last of his energy reserves and bursting through the door, stirring heavy debris off the ground into a gray haze. Rebecca was holding herself in a ball amid heaps of broken glass and ceramic.

"Rebecca, what—"

"You were right, Caleb," she wailed. "You were right."

He dropped down to her level and brought his shattered wife into his arms.

"You were right," she whimpered again into his shoulder.

"What happened in here?"

"I thought about what you said. I wanted to clean it up a little. For *him*. I wanted to clean it up and I—oh God. Caleb, the shelf came down. The *whole shelf*. And I don't know how to find him. It all just looks like dust."

About the Authors

Lee Sloan is an author, filmmaker, musician, and voice actor who teaches high school English and creative writing. He enjoys survival horror games, specifically the Resident Evil series, and almost exclusively watches horror films. Lee won the Most Vile Villain award at a film festival for a short film he wrote and directed in which he portrayed a serial killer. When he isn't working on creative projects, he can be found playing Pokémon Go with friends or watching one of the many Walking Dead spin-offs.

Adian Suvic is an author, English teacher, and student pilot working towards becoming a captain. He fell in love with writing in elementary school and believes creativity is the foundation for a fulfilling life. When he isn't flying or writing, Adian is usually playing fighting games, trying to replicate Evo Moment #37.

Aaron Joiner graduated in 2020 with his MA in English from the University of North Florida and has spent much of his time as a writer pondering and exploring themes of identity, sexuality, and social introspection. Inspired by the strange, obscure, and fantastical, he enjoys writing stories that challenge the habits of his own body of work and the notion of what a story can be. He currently teaches high school English.

www.ingramcontent.com/pod-product-compliance
Lightning Source LLC
Chambersburg PA
CBHW052012240626
47153CB00008B/2842